OXFORD WORLD'S CLASSICS

KEW GARDENS AND OTHER SHORT FICTION

BRYONY RANDALL is Professor of Modernist Literature, University of Glasgow. She is co-General Editor with Jane Goldman and Susan Sellers of the Cambridge edition of the works of Virginia Woolf, and volume editor of the *Collected Short Fiction* for that edition. Her publications include *Modernism, Daily Time and Everyday Life* (2007) and, as co-editor with Jane Goldman, the collection of essays *Virginia Woolf in Context* (2013).

OXFORD WORLD'S CLASSICS

*For over 100 years Oxford World's Classics have brought
readers closer to the world's great literature. Now with over 700
titles—from the 4,000-year-old myths of Mesopotamia to the
twentieth century's greatest novels—the series makes available
lesser-known as well as celebrated writing.*

*The pocket-sized hardbacks of the early years contained
introductions by Virginia Woolf, T. S. Eliot, Graham Greene,
and other literary figures which enriched the experience of reading.
Today the series is recognized for its fine scholarship and
reliability in texts that span world literature, drama and poetry,
religion, philosophy, and politics. Each edition includes perceptive
commentary and essential background information to meet the
changing needs of readers.*

OXFORD WORLD'S CLASSICS

VIRGINIA WOOLF

Kew Gardens and Other Short Fiction

Edited with an Introduction and Notes by
BRYONY RANDALL

OXFORD
UNIVERSITY PRESS

OXFORD
UNIVERSITY PRESS

Great Clarendon Street, Oxford, OX2 6DP,
United Kingdom

Oxford University Press is a department of the University of Oxford.
It furthers the University's objective of excellence in research, scholarship,
and education by publishing worldwide. Oxford is a registered trade mark of
Oxford University Press in the UK and in certain other countries

First published as an Oxford World's Classics paperback 2022

Impression: 3

Published in the United States of America by Oxford University Press
198 Madison Avenue, New York, NY 10016, United States of America

British Library Cataloguing in Publication Data

Data available

Library of Congress Control Number: 2022931922

ISBN 978–0–19–883813–5

Printed and bound in Great Britain by
Clays Ltd, Elcograf S.p.A.

CONTENTS

KEW GARDENS AND OTHER
SHORT FICTION

BIOGRAPHICAL PREFACE

VIRGINIA WOOLF was born Adeline Virginia Stephen on 25 January 1882 at 22 Hyde Park Gate, Kensington. Her father, Leslie Stephen, himself a widower, had married in 1878 Julia Jackson, widow of Herbert Duckworth. Between them they already had four children; a fifth, Vanessa, was born in 1879, a sixth, Thoby, in 1880. There followed Virginia and, in 1883, Adrian.

Both of the parents had strong family associations with literature. Leslie Stephen was the son of Sir James Stephen, a noted historian, and brother of Sir James Fitzjames Stephen, a distinguished lawyer and writer on law. His first wife was a daughter of Thackeray, his second had been an admired associate of the Pre-Raphaelites, and also, like her first husband, had aristocratic connections. Stephen himself is best remembered as the founding editor of the *Dictionary of National Biography*, and as an alpinist, but he was also a remarkable journalist, biographer, and historian of ideas; his *History of English Thought in the Eighteenth Century* (1876) is still of great value. No doubt our strongest idea of him derives from the character of Mr Ramsay in *To the Lighthouse*; for a less impressionistic portrait, which conveys a strong sense of his centrality in the intellectual life of the time, one can consult Noël Annan's *Leslie Stephen* (revised edition, 1984).

Virginia had the free run of her father's library, a better substitute for the public school and university education she was denied than most women of the time could aspire to; her brothers, of course, were sent to Clifton and Westminster. Her mother died in 1895, and in that year she had her first breakdown, possibly related in some way to the sexual molestation of which her half-brother George Duckworth is accused. By 1897 she was able to read again, and did so voraciously: 'Gracious, child, how you gobble', remarked her father, who, with a liberality and good sense at odds with the age in which they lived, allowed her to choose her reading freely. In other respects her relationship with her father was difficult; his deafness and melancholy, his excessive emotionalism, not helped by successive bereavements, all increased her nervousness.

Stephen fell ill in 1902 and died in 1904. Virginia suffered another breakdown, during which she heard the birds singing in Greek, a language in which she had acquired some competence. On her recovery she moved, with her brothers and sister, to a house in Gordon Square, Bloomsbury; there, and subsequently at several other nearby addresses, what eventually became famous as the Bloomsbury Group took shape.

Virginia had long considered herself a writer. It was in 1905 that she began to write for publication in the *Times Literary Supplement*. In her circle (more loosely drawn than is sometimes supposed) were many whose names are now half-forgotten, but some were or became famous: J. M. Keynes and E. M. Forster and Roger Fry; also Clive Bell, who married Vanessa, Lytton Strachey, who once proposed marriage to her, and Leonard Woolf. Despite much ill health in these years, she travelled a good deal, and had an interesting social life in London. She did a little adult-education teaching, worked for female suffrage, and shared the excitement of Roger Fry's Post-Impressionist Exhibition in 1910. In 1912, after another bout of nervous illness, she married Leonard Woolf.

She was thirty, and had not yet published a book, though *The Voyage Out* was in preparation. It was accepted for publication by her half-brother Gerald Duckworth in 1913 (it appeared in 1915). She was often ill with depression and anorexia, and in 1913 attempted suicide. But after a bout of violent madness her health seemed to settle down, and in 1917 a printing press was installed at Hogarth House, Richmond, where she and her husband were living. The Hogarth Press, later an illustrious institution, but at first meant in part as therapy for Virginia, was now inaugurated. She began *Night and Day*, and finished it in 1918. It was published by Duckworth in 1919, the year in which the Woolfs bought Monk's House, Rodmell, for £700. There, in 1920, she began *Jacob's Room*, finished, and published by the Woolfs' own Hogarth Press, in 1922. In the following year she began *Mrs Dalloway* (finished in 1924, published 1925), when she was already working on *To the Lighthouse* (finished and published, after intervals of illness, in 1927). *Orlando*, a fantastic 'biography' of a man–woman, and a tribute to Virginia's close friendship with Vita Sackville-West, was written quite rapidly over the winter of 1927–8, and published, with considerable success, in October. *The Waves* was written and rewritten in 1930 and 1931 (published in October of that year). She had already started on *Flush*, the story of Elizabeth Barrett Browning's pet dog—another success with the public—and in 1932 began work on what became *The Years*.

This brief account of her work during the first twenty years of her marriage is of course incomplete; she had also written and published many shorter works, as well as both series of *The Common Reader*, and *A Room of One's Own*. There have been accounts of the marriage very hostile to Leonard Woolf, but he can hardly be accused of cramping her talent or hindering the development of her career.

The Years proved an agonizingly difficult book to finish, and was completely rewritten at least twice. Her friend Roger Fry having died in 1934, she planned to write a biography, but illnesses in 1936 delayed the project; towards the end of that year she began instead the polemical *Three Guineas*, published in 1938. *The Years* had meanwhile appeared in 1937, by which time she was again at work on the Fry biography, and already sketching in her head the book that was to be *Between the Acts*. *Roger Fry* was published in the terrifying summer of 1940. By the autumn of that year many of the familiar Bloomsbury houses had been destroyed or badly damaged by bombs. Back at Monk's House, she worked on *Between the Acts*, and finished it in February 1941. Thereafter her mental condition deteriorated alarmingly, and on 28 March, unable to face another bout of insanity, she drowned herself in the River Ouse.

Her career as a writer of fiction covers the years 1912–41, thirty years distracted by intermittent serious illness as well as by the demands, which she regarded as very important, of family and friends, and by the need or desire to write literary criticism and social comment. Her industry was extraordinary—nine highly-wrought novels, two or three of them among the great masterpieces of the form in this century, along with all the other writings, including the copious journals and letters that have been edited and published in recent years. Firmly set though her life was in the 'Bloomsbury' context—the agnostic ethic transformed from that of her forebears, the influence of G. E. Moore and the Cambridge Apostles, the individual brilliance of J. M. Keynes, Strachey, Forster, and the others—we have come more and more to value the distinctiveness of her talent, so that she seems more and more to stand free of any context that might be thought to limit her. None of that company—except, perhaps, T. S. Eliot, who was on the fringe of it—did more to establish the possibilities of literary innovation, or to demonstrate that such innovation must be

brought about by minds familiar with the innovations of the past.
This is true originality. It was Eliot who said of *Jacob's Room* that in
that book she had freed herself from any compromise between the
traditional novel and her original gift; it was the freedom he himself
sought in *The Waste Land*, published in the same year, a freedom that
was dependent upon one's knowing with intimacy that with which
compromise must be avoided, so that the knowledge became part of
the originality. In fact she had 'gobbled' her father's books to a higher
purpose than he could have understood.

Frank Kermode

INTRODUCTION

IT is not widely known that Virginia Woolf, a groundbreaking experimental novelist who during her career reinvented the form several times over, was also writing short fiction almost continuously from childhood—'All through her life, Virginia Woolf used at intervals to write short stories', her husband Leonard explained.[1] But only a small proportion—at most, one-fifth—of the short fiction Woolf wrote was published in her lifetime. The best-known of these pieces are celebrated for their play with perspective; for their attempts to evoke fleeting emotions and profound interiority; and for their radical attempts to convey the visual through the verbal. But her short fictions are also by turns political, cynical, melancholy, comic, or empathetic; they take us to fantastical exotic landscapes, haunted houses, the depths of flower beds or middle-class drawing rooms; their narrative voices may be intimate, jolly, acerbic, tender, or so diffuse that their presence is barely discernible. Each piece startles in its own way: through the intimate snail's-eye view of 'Kew Gardens' or the robust satire of 'A Society'; the barbed compassion of 'The New Dress' or the hallucinatory synaesthesia of 'Monday or Tuesday'. And this extraordinary variety is in itself startling, like that in evidence among the detritus collected by the protagonist of Woolf's story 'Solid Objects':

The contrast between the china so vivid and alert, and the glass so mute and contemplative, fascinated him [. . .] he asked himself how the two came to exist in the same world, let alone to stand upon the same narrow strip of marble in the same room. The question remained unanswered. (p. 29)

The contrasts between some of Woolf's short fictions, likewise, lead one to ask how they came to exist in the same body of work.

While there is no single answer to this question, part of the reason for the variety in Woolf's short fiction lies in the longevity of her engagement with the form. Woolf began writing short fiction as a child, contributing comic stories such as 'A Cockney's Farming Experiences' to the Stephen family's publication *The Hyde Park Gate News* (composed by Virginia, these stories were often written out by

[1] Leonard Woolf, 'Foreword', *A Haunted House* (London: Hogarth Press, 1944), 7.

her older sister Vanessa—owing, presumably, to the latter's superior penmanship). A dozen or so short fiction manuscripts survive dating from around 1906 to 1910; there is then a break in the archive (though not necessarily in her writing) before the composition of 'The Mark on the Wall'. This, Woolf's first published short fiction, appeared in 1917 in *Two Stories*, itself the first publication by the Hogarth Press, which was owned and operated by the Woolfs (the other story in that publication was 'Three Jews' by Leonard, himself a Jew). This marked the start of Woolf's most concentrated period of short fiction writing, including the publication of *Monday or Tuesday* in 1921, again by the Hogarth Press; *Monday or Tuesday* would be the only short story collection that Woolf published in her lifetime. However, Woolf continued writing short fictions throughout the early 1920s, and while many of these were crucial to the development of her novels published in this period (*Jacob's Room* in 1922, and *Mrs Dalloway* in 1925), a number were stand-alone pieces, such as the enchanting children's stories 'The Widow and the Parrot: A True Story' and 'Nurse Lugton's Curtains'. What is more, short fictions related to her novels were not necessarily abandoned as preparatory pieces once the novels were published. For example, Woolf worked extensively on a number of stories set at Mrs Dalloway's party for some time after that novel was published—including 'The New Dress', which appears in this collection.[2] By the late 1920s, Woolf was sufficiently well known that high-circulation magazines were inviting her to write short fiction for publication; according to Leonard, Woolf kept a drawer of short stories in draft form, and 'if an editor asked her for a short story, and she felt in the mood to write one (which was not frequent), she would take a sketch out of her drawer and rewrite it, sometimes a great many times'.[3] But there are very many more short fictions in manuscript or typescript form than were actually published. What may be the last piece of fiction that Woolf ever wrote is a short piece called 'The Watering Place', typed up and revised by Woolf in February 1941; she died in March of that year.

'The short story', Woolf's biographer Julia Briggs argued, 'remained for Woolf a place for experiment and an occasion for learning—their

---

[2] Most, though not all, of these stories were published in the collection *Mrs Dalloway's Party*, ed. Stella McNichol (London: Hogarth Press, 1973).

[3] Leonard Woolf, 'Foreword', 7.

value was primarily for her, rather than for her readers.'[4] Indeed, much has been made of Woolf's apparent dismissal of some of the pieces she included in *Monday or Tuesday* in a letter to her friend Ethel Smyth written in 1930. There she describes the thrill that short fiction composition gave her, particularly in the late 1910s when she was working on (and struggling with) her novel *Night and Day* (1919):

These little pieces [. . .] were written by way of diversion; they were the treats I allowed myself when I had done my exercise in the conventional style [working on *Night and Day*]. I shall never forget the day I wrote The Mark on the Wall—all in a flash, as if flying, after being kept stone breaking for months. The Unwritten Novel was the great discovery, however. That—again in one second—showed me how I could embody all my deposit of experience in a shape that fitted it [. . .] How I trembled with excitement; and then Leonard came in, and I drank my milk, and concealed my excitement[5]

While looking fondly on stories such as 'The Mark on the Wall', 'Kew Gardens', and 'An Unwritten Novel', she describes 'Green and blue and the heron one ["Monday or Tuesday"]' as 'mere tangles of words'. Later, however, she adds a further layer of commentary, calling these two pieces 'wild outbursts of freedom, inarticulate, ridiculous, unprintable mere outcries'.[6] Embedded in her negative appraisal of these pieces, then, is the term 'freedom', and the freedom which the short story form offered Woolf is clear from the selection of works included in this edition. While long recognized as a form in which she tried out some of her more experimental techniques before adopting and adapting them for use in her novel-length work, Woolf's short fictions are now widely appreciated as important works of art in their own right, rather than simply flights of fancy awaiting their full actualization in the novel form; their value to readers becomes clearer on each rereading. This collection focuses on the most productive period of short fiction writing in Woolf's life, the late 1910s through to the end of the 1920s. It includes all eight stories which make up *Monday or Tuesday*, and six further stories spanning the period 1920 to 1929, published in journals, collections, or magazines. Taken as

[4] Julia Briggs, *Virginia Woolf: An Inner Life* (London: Penguin, 2005), 81.
[5] *The Letters of Virginia Woolf*, ed. Nigel Nicolson and Joanne Trautmann (6 vols; London: Hogarth Press, 1975–80), iv. 231.
[6] *Letters*, iv. 231.

a whole, this collection puts before its readers some of the most innovative works that Woolf ever produced.

'A Case of Atmosphere': The Verbal and the Visual

Despite Woolf's own later reservations, the fact that she did see the stories collected here through to publication demonstrates that we ought to treat them with the respect they deserve, as fully formed artworks. One crucial context here, helping us to understand the way in which Woolf conceived of these short fictions at the time of writing, is the original physical form in which the works were first published. The relationship between verbal and visual art reached a particularly significant phase in the early twentieth century, when artists and writers looking for novel ways of presenting their experience of a rapidly changing and newly understood world often sought inspiration from other media. Woolf's own short fictions of the 1910s and early 1920s often flicker around a central image or images—primarily visual, though often engaging the other senses—impressionistically gathering up ideas, emotions, and sensual responses. It is no surprise that among the most enthusiastic early admirers of her short fiction was Woolf's friend the vanguard art critic and painter Roger Fry, who coined the term 'post-impressionist' for the experimental art movement he championed: praising 'The Mark on the Wall', he singled her out as the only writer making 'the texture of the words have a meaning and quality really almost apart from what you are talking about'.[7] What is more, print culture was flourishing, with developments in print and distribution technologies making for a proliferation in small presses, magazines, and journals, meeting the appetites of an increasingly literate and sophisticated reading audience.[8] Reflecting on the original material form in which they appeared— taking note of what the critic Jerome McGann calls the 'bibliographic code' of these publications—sheds important light on the aesthetic and cultural context into which these stories were born.[9]

[7] Roger Fry to Virginia Woolf, 18 October 1918, cited by Frances Spalding, *Roger Fry: Art and Life* (Berkeley and Los Angeles: University of California Press, 1980), 212.

[8] For more on this topic, see Faye Hammill and Mark Hussey, *Modernism's Print Cultures* (London: Bloomsbury, 2016).

[9] Jerome McGann, 'What Is Critical Editing?', in McGann, *The Textual Condition* (Princeton: Princeton University Press, 1991), 48–68, at 56.

The first edition of 'Kew Gardens', this collection's title story, exemplifies the intimate relationship between the visual and the verbal in the aesthetic of the period. The Hogarth Press had already signalled its commitment to integrating these art forms in its first publication, *Two Stories*, which included woodcuts by the artist Dora Carrington. *Kew Gardens*, the press's second publication, was, like *Two Stories*, printed by hand. The story appeared as a slim sixteen-page volume of its own, beautifully bound in handmade wrappers of paper patterned with blue, dark brown, and orange, making each copy unique; the wrappers were made at the Omega Workshops, an avant-garde creative enterprise overseen by Roger Fry. Even more significantly, the pamphlet was the first in a number of collaborations between Woolf and her sister, the artist Vanessa Bell. As Julia Briggs suggests, 'Vanessa had long before abandoned surface realism to concentrate on the impact of form and structure in painting. Her approach, and the theories that underwrote it, helped Virginia to make her own art "new".'[10] Woolf sent Vanessa a draft of 'Kew Gardens' in July 1918; describing it as 'a case of atmosphere', she also asked if Vanessa might 'design a title page' for the story.[11] Bell clearly suggested she might make some woodcuts, since Woolf later responded that were she to do so 'I don't see that it matters whether it's about the story or not',[12] reinforcing the sense that Bell's contributions were to be understood as artworks in their own right, responding to the 'atmosphere' of, rather than (necessarily) literally representing, Woolf's text. A fortnight later, Vanessa had made a first drawing and Woolf found it 'just in the mood I wanted'.[13] The rapturous review which ensured the success of *Kew Gardens* specifically praised it as 'a thing of original and therefore strange beauty, with its own "atmosphere", its own vital force'.[14]

Bell eventually made two woodcuts for the first edition of *Kew Gardens*. The first, which appeared as a frontispiece, depicts two women whose fluid, organic shapes blend with the garden scenery behind them. The second, at the end of the story, features a caterpillar, and a moth or butterfly—perhaps two from different angles. The perspectives of these woodcuts, therefore, reverse the trajectory of

---

[10] Briggs, *Virginia Woolf*, 68.   [11] *Letters*, ii. 257.   [12] *Letters*, ii. 258.
[13] *Letters*, ii. 259.
[14] 'Kew Gardens', *Times Literary Supplement*, 29 May 1919, 293.

the narrative in the story itself, which begins with a forensic investigation of the progress of a snail through a flower bed, and ends with a panoramic vision of London 'like a vast nest of Chinese boxes all of wrought steel turning ceaselessly one within another' (p. 15). The juxtaposition of this mechanical, expansive vision—albeit one tempered by Woolf's final invocation of 'petals of myriads of flowers' (p. 15)—with Bell's closing image, whose design makes parts of these insects apparently flow into each other, returns the reader's mind to the opening of the story, reinforcing the piece's cyclical structure and its grounding in the organic rhythms of nature; the 'form and structure' emphasized in Bell's own visual aesthetic is foregrounded. Woolf's inclusion of her sister's art in her publication was not merely a decorative addition: bound together in a single volume, these artworks drive home the value of close attention to all the senses, in particular the visual, and what such close attention reveals about humanity's inextricable relationship with non-human nature.

'Kew Gardens' was republished three further times in Woolf's lifetime, and each time in a volume including illustrations by Bell. Such was its popularity on publication, it was republished in June 1919, again with Bell's two woodcuts—although not, this time, printed by the Hogarth Press themselves; Bell had objected to the quality of the reproductions of the woodcuts in the first edition. Her concerns were well founded. The third appearance of 'Kew Gardens' was in *Monday or Tuesday*, and Bell produced four new woodcuts for this collection (although none illustrate 'Kew Gardens' directly). The technical challenge of printing text interspersed with images was, it seems, a step too far for the relatively unsophisticated technology of the Hogarth Press; the same reviewer who had been so enthusiastic about 'Kew Gardens', while praising *Monday or Tuesday*, observed that the collection was marred by ink from the woodcuts marking the pages opposite, or showing through the pages on which they were printed.[15] Leonard Woolf admitted that *Monday or Tuesday* was 'one of the worst printed books ever published'.[16] And yet, there is something entirely apt about the literal overlaying of the images and the stories in this collection, which continue Woolf's experimentation with structure and form, her exploration of the dialogue between the

---

[15] 'Monday or Tuesday', *Times Literary Supplement*, 7 April 1921, 227.
[16] Leonard Woolf, *An Autobiography* (Oxford: Oxford University Press, 1980), ii. 174.

visual and the verbal—perhaps most obviously in the word picture 'Blue & Green' whose layout on the page even echoes the appearance of two framed artworks hanging side by side. To complete the story of 'Kew Gardens': its final publication in Woolf's lifetime, in 1927, featured an even fuller integration with the visual: the cover and title page were designed by Bell, and her artwork—described as 'decoration'—adorned each page of the story, framing and sometimes intertwining with the text itself.

While the Hogarth Press, particularly in its early days, may not always have been able to generate a finished product of the highest material quality, the benefit to Woolf of absolute control over how her work appeared, including which images (if any) appeared alongside her text, is clear. In a letter written in July 1917 she says 'its [*sic*] very amusing to try with these short things, and the greatest mercy to be able to do what one likes—no editors, or publishers'.[17] When her work was published elsewhere, the juxtaposition of text and image was not always so harmonious. Woolf's 1929 story 'The Lady in the Looking-Glass: A Reflection', was first published in *Harper's Magazine*, a US-based literary journal, in December 1929, with no illustration. It was republished under the slightly different title 'In the Looking-Glass' in the glossy fashion magazine *Harper's Bazaar* a month later. The *Harper's Bazaar* version was prefaced by a large illustration by the celebrated photographer and interior and stage designer Cecil Beaton. The illustration shows a woman—the story's protagonist Isabella Tyson—reflected in a mirror, along with various items lying on a hall table. The story does not give a physical description of Isabella, but cautions that the narrator's own temptation to describe her in terms of the elegant garden in which she appears is misguided: 'for it is impossible that any woman of flesh and blood of fifty-five or sixty should be really a wreath or a tendril' (p. 76). And yet, this accurately describes how Beaton's illustration depicts her: willowy, graceful—and, implicitly, intellectual, surrounded as she is in the illustration (though not in the story) by the markers of high culture. The illustration features the letters which are left on the table by a postman halfway through the story, but none of the other items Beaton depicted, which include several books, a pair of spectacles, and a small nude sculpture, are mentioned in the story. While Woolf did not herself insist on direct representation of the content of her fiction in any accompanying illustration—as the exchange with Vanessa about 'Kew Gardens' illustrates—nevertheless she clearly aimed for sympathetic rendition of the atmosphere, tone, or mood. Here, the illustration appears to offer a direct representation of a scene from the story, but does so in a way that not only misrepresents the story's content but also misjudges the story's tone. As the critic Alice Wood has observed, the illustration, together with the editorial insertion of a subtitle and epigraph emphasizing the dreamlike quality of the story, 'seems to dress up Woolf as Isabella',[18] in the guise of a highbrow socialite, whereas in fact the story's power lies in its critique of the superficial sophistication of the social group Isabella represents. Woolf did not appear to be aware of this illustration—or if she was, she did not mention it when asking her friends whether she ought to agree to be photographed by Beaton, first in 1927 and again in 1930. She refused on both occasions and was furious when she discovered he had included an image of her in his 1930 publication *The Book of Beauty* without her permission—later describing him as 'that bloody bounder Beaton'.[19]

Woolf was extremely sensitive about the circulation of images of herself—she hated sitting for photographs and portraits—which makes it all the more remarkable that she apparently agreed to have her 1926 story 'A Woman's College from Outside' appear in print alongside a photograph of herself. The story was published in *Atalanta's Garland: Being the Book of the Edinburgh University Women's Union*—a very different context from the glossy high-circulation *Harper's Bazaar*. This story was originally drafted as a chapter of Woolf's 1922 novel *Jacob's Room*, but did not appear in the final publication. Instead, its only print incarnation in Woolf's lifetime had it appear alongside work by numerous other celebrated literary figures of the period, including Katherine Mansfield, Hilaire Belloc, Walter de la Mare, and Naomi Mitchison—putting her in illustrious company, as befitted her own status by this time. The portrait which Woolf presumably suggested (or agreed) for inclusion was, however, originally taken for the fashion magazine *Vogue* in 1924, and appeared

---

[18] Alice Wood, 'Modernism, Exclusivity, and the Sophisticated Public of Harper's Bazaar (UK)', *Modernist Cultures*, 11/3 (November 2016), 370–88, at 379.

[19] *Letters*, iv. 375.

as part of its 'We Nominate for the Hall of Fame' feature. In this portrait, Woolf wears a dress of her mother's, dating back many decades (Woolf's mother died in 1895, when Woolf was 13). Woolf had in fact sat for the same photographers in 1925 in contemporary dress, so her decision to permit the use of this particular photograph to illustrate her story is notable, presenting Woolf as someone deeply attached to her past, through the maternal line, and emphatically not a fly-by-night celebrity concerned with her own image. It was not that Woolf was uninterested in fashion and the party set; indeed, she was ambivalently drawn to it.[20] Reflecting on that 1925 photo shoot, Woolf recorded that 'I should like to investigate the party consciousness, the frock consciousness &c.'[21] The fruits of that interest can be seen in 'The New Dress', published a couple of years later, where the self-conscious protagonist also opts to wear the fashion of a previous generation, resulting in agonized social embarrassment vying with flashes of determination and self-awareness. It is just such an awareness of the social significance of clothing that we discern in the juxtaposition of 'A Woman's College from Outside' with a photograph of a soberly dressed, old-fashioned Woolf, which implicitly asks us to read the piece with a certain seriousness; the tone evoked would be quite different had the story been accompanied by an image of Woolf as (fashionable) celebrity.

'A Woman's College from Outside' is, as the title suggests, profoundly concerned with the nexus of gender and education—making it, of course, particularly suitable for inclusion in the *Atalanta's Garland* collection. The story's soft, moonlit setting draws the reader gently into a world in which the injustices of economic inequality, and the hypocrisy of the sexual double standard, permeate young women's experience of higher education—for those lucky enough to have access to it. Woolf's fullest exploration of these themes is to be found in her long essay *A Room of One's Own* (1929)—originally written to be delivered as two lectures to the students of the all-female Newnham College, Cambridge. The seeds of this powerful attack on patriarchy, whose impact is still felt nearly one hundred years after its

[20] For a full exploration of this topic, see Randi Koppen, *Virginia Woolf, Fashion and Literary Modernity* (Edinburgh: Edinburgh University Press, 2009).

[21] *The Diary of Virginia Woolf*, ed. Anne Olivier Bell and Andrew McNeillie (5 vols; London: Hogarth Press, 1977–84), iii. 12.

publication, are clearly present in 'A Woman's College from Outside'. Had this story appeared in *Jacob's Room* it would have been a brief parallel, by way of contrast, to the protagonist Jacob's experience as a young man at a Cambridge college. Appearing in an organ devoted to women's education, and accompanied by a portrait of the author which pays homage to her maternal inheritance, these young women's stories are literally given their own space.

'How Readily Our Thoughts Swarm upon a New Object'

Woolf was deeply aware of the impact of the material appearance of texts, not least because of her experience as a publisher and printer—she hand set a number of the Hogarth Press's early publications herself. We get a wonderful glimpse of her feeling for the materiality of words in 'Kew Gardens': not only is a list of foodstuffs rendered on the page as a poem of sorts, but one of the participants in that conversation 'looked through the pattern of falling words [. . .] letting the words fall over her' (p. 13). Books, pamphlets, magazines, and journals were part of her life not only as means of conveying ideas and feelings, but also as tangible objects, which—as the tragicomic story of the printing of *Monday or Tuesday* attests—frequently resist or frustrate the control of the humans with whom they come into contact. The narrator of 'The Lady in the Looking-Glass' reflects on the potency of objects more generally, their apparent capacity to have agency or even consciousness: 'Sometimes it seemed as if they [the objects Isabella has collected from around the world] knew more about her than we, who sat on them, wrote at them, and trod on them so carefully, were allowed to know' (p. 76). To this extent, they appear less as objects and more as 'things', as the term has been (re)defined in recent years: 'vivid entities not entirely reducible to the contexts in which (human) subjects set them'.[22]

Woolf's short fictions are replete with objects—or indeed, things—whose purpose is unclear, whose meaning ambiguous, or whose impact on human life apparently disproportionate to their conventional significance. Woolf's first published short story, 'The Mark on the Wall', is a 3,000-word reverie on a minuscule, indeterminate,

---

[22] Jane Bennett, *Vibrant Matter: A Political Ecology of Things* (Durham, NC: Duke University Press, 2010), 5.

domestic object—very possibly, in fact, some detritus that might not normally even be recognized as an independent entity. 'How readily our thoughts swarm upon a new object,' the narrator of this story muses, 'lifting it a little way, as ants carry a blade of straw so feverishly, and then leave it . . .' (p. 3). The story itself, accordingly, follows the narrator's mental process, picking up and dropping its concerns abruptly. It roams across millennia, and across continents, taking in prehistoric burial grounds and London's Kingsway; Shakespeare and housemaids; underground trains, ancient Troy, and brown-paper parcels. This apparently indiscriminate attention is the key formal quality of this story, and also sketches out the story's subtle but powerful politics. The whole piece is about the power of rules, and about resisting rules—including the rules of how a short story should be written. The story's initial focus on material objects, its grounding in a very specific domestic scene featuring a book, chrysanthemums, and cigarette, moving swiftly to the reflection on lost objects (to which surely any reader can relate), offers a kind of gesture of solidarity with the reader: we all know, see, touch real objects, we all share the same material world—although, as the story will suggest, our individual access to and experiences of that world may be very different. But while acknowledging the comfort to be found in the material—the narrator recalls, to recover from a moment of existential angst, 'worshipping the chest of drawers, worshipping solidity, worshipping reality' (p. 8)—the story also reminds us of the impermanence of material objects. Dust, which we and all things will eventually become, explicitly and implicitly permeates the story.

It is against this fundamentally levelling backdrop that Woolf mocks the imposition of hierarchies, most strikingly in the repeated reference to Whitaker's Table of Precedency, an annual handbook setting out the social hierarchy of the United Kingdom. The notion of human beings, all made of dust, giving themselves pompous titles in order to finely calibrate their social station ('The Archbishop of Canterbury is followed by the Lord High Chancellor; the Lord High Chancellor is followed by the Archbishop of York', p. 8) becomes, in this context, farcical. The absurdity of social rules and strictures is crystallized in the story's commentary on tablecloths:

The rule for tablecloths at that particular period was that they should be made of tapestry with little yellow compartments marked upon them, such as you may see in photographs of the carpets in the corridors of the royal palaces. Tablecloths of a different kind were not real tablecloths. (p. 6)

Woolf takes the principles of Whitaker's Table of Precedency to its logical conclusion—that everyone, and everything, must comply with the 'rule' and know their socially defined place. Therefore, if a certain object does not comply with the narrow definition of how it ought to appear, it can apparently no longer be categorized as what it manifestly is—indeed it might no longer qualify as an object at all: 'not real tablecloths'. Woolf's own circuitous, anticlimactic, domestic, cerebral short story, with its tonal mix of frivolity and pointed social critique, takes pride in its own failure to comply with existing conventional definitions of what a short story should be—in, perhaps, being 'not a real short story'. In one banal sense, the story does eventually answer what is notionally its central question—what is that mark on the wall? But *en route* it asks many more questions: about our material and social world, about cognition, about art itself.

One of the central questions 'The Mark on the Wall' implicitly asks is 'how important are material things?'—and the question remains open. On the one hand, they are mocked, blown into dust. On the other, a material object was the prompt for the story itself, the reason for its very existence. Throughout, these short fictions display an ambivalence about attachments to material objects. The title of 'Solid Objects' purports to offer us a grounding in solidity; in the stable, immutable, and coherent. In fact, this story's exploration of a young man's mysterious obsession with the things other people throw away implies that these items are meaningless, superfluous, damaged, and thus repellent; and yet at the same time meaningful, beautiful, complete, and fundamental. It is tempting to take at face value the narrator's observation that 'any object mixes itself so profoundly with the stuff of thought that it loses its actual form and recomposes itself a little differently in an ideal shape which haunts the brain when we least expect it' (p. 28)—in other words, objects change according to the intellectual and emotional meaning ascribed to them by the humans around them. But it is quite clear from the meticulousness with which John sifts the city's detritus, with which he arranges the objects that apparently fulfil a deep, if inarticulable, need in him (deeper, we note, than the need for approval from institutions offering social power and prestige) that each object is valued for, and retains, its significant 'actual form'.

'A Haunted House' plays with one of the most familiar cultural tropes of a material thing which evades (living) human control; which takes on, literally, a life (or lives) of its own. The house in this story is, in common with those in many haunted-house stories, anthropomorphized, blurring the boundaries between the animate and the inanimate. 'The pulse of the house' beats throughout the story, the word 'pulse' occurring five times in its two short pages—as if the story itself were also alive, driven by this beating rhythm. The life of the story also comes from the tension between the static objects by which the reader attempts to navigate this domestic space—the apples, windowpanes, a book, carpet, candle, lamp—and the fluidity of the pronouns it uses: the first three paragraphs use 'you', 'they', 'she', 'he', 'we', and 'one', sliding from one to the next in a refusal of any stable narrative position. What is haunting about this house is not so much that an object which ought to be inanimate is alive; it is that the reader is given no stable position from which to assess what is solid, tangible, earthly, and what is imagined, other-worldly, ethereal. An even more extreme version of this instability is found in perhaps Woolf's most abstract published work, 'Blue & Green'. Even before reading the texts themselves, the reader is unsettled by the fact that the order in which the two pieces appear on the page is the reverse of that announced in the title. While this foregrounds the materiality of type, of marks on the page, and thus the page as an object, the pieces themselves give us very little grounding in materiality. 'Green' ostensibly describes a specific object—an ornament made of glass called a lustre—but the language takes us across rainforests, deserts, and oceans, literally and intellectually thousands of miles from a middle-class mantelpiece. And the apparent object of 'Blue'—a lively 'snub-nosed monster' (p. 37) and his immediate environment—are comprised of the inanimate (beads, tarpaulin, pebbles), eventually swept away by the waves of the story to have a vast, cold, inert space take their place.

Back in the drawing rooms of the middle class—which fascinated Woolf her whole life, having had the arcane social rules of tea-time 'at home' govern her childhood—we find a number of these stories giving serious consideration to an aspect of material life often belittled or sneered at by patriarchal society: namely, clothing. The astonishing hypocrisy of male attitudes to women's interest in dress was skewered by Woolf in a footnote to her 1938 polemic *Three Guineas*:

The fact that both sexes have a very marked though dissimilar love of dress seems to have escaped the notice of the dominant sex owing largely it must be supposed to the hypnotic power of dominance. Thus the late Mr Justice MacCardie, in summing up the case of Mrs Frankau, remarked: 'Women cannot be expected to renounce an essential feature of femininity or to abandon one of nature's solaces for a constant and insuperable physical handicap . . . Dress, after all, is one of the chief methods of women's self-expression . . . In matters of dress women often remain children to the end. The psychology of the matter must not be overlooked. But whilst bearing the above matters in mind the law has rightly laid it down that the rule of prudence and proportion must be observed.' The Judge who thus dictated was wearing a scarlet robe, an ermine cape, and a vast wig of artificial curls.[23]

While the tilt at men's hypocrisy is, in this extract, clear, the overall attitude to clothing expressed in Woolf's work is far from straightforward. In *Three Guineas*, she might equally be seen to be defending the importance of dress, or mocking both Mrs Frankau and Mr Justice MacCardie's attachment to it. But the attention that her short fiction pays to clothing suggests that, while Woolf may sometimes regret the judgements made about a person based on their dress, the fact that it is a legitimate 'method [. . .] of self-expression' is unarguable. 'The New Dress', as noted earlier, is a key example of Woolf's investigation of 'the frock consciousness'—'consciousness' being a particularly apt word in relation to this story, which centres on the mental and emotional distress Mabel experiences on realizing that her experiment with dress has been—according to those who judge her at the party—a failure. Rather than being admired for her bold rejection of fashion, she is mocked for it. As Woolf puts it later in the *Three Guineas* footnote, 'Singularity of dress, when not associated with office, seldom escapes ridicule'. And yet, while the narrative focus of 'The New Dress' clearly aligns the reader's empathy with Mabel, we are also well able to recognize the absurd figure she appears to cut; we, too, are tempted into the *Schadenfreude* of ridiculing her. Compare the 'narrow and long and fashionable' shoes of Isabella Tyson in 'The Lady in the Looking-Glass': 'Like everything she wore, they were

[23] Virginia Woolf, *Three Guineas* (1938; London: Hogarth Press, 1986), 169–70 n. 16.

exquisite' (p. 78), the narrator observes, and it is much more alluring to put ourselves into those shoes than imagine ourselves in Mabel's awkward position.

Implicitly contrasting the elegance of Mrs Dalloway's drawing room with the 'hot, stuffy, sordid' workroom of her dressmaker Miss Milan brings Mabel a sudden realization:

she felt, suddenly, honestly, full of love for Miss Milan, much, much fonder of Miss Milan than of any one in the whole world, and could have cried for pity that she should be crawling on the floor with her mouth full of pins, and her face red and her eyes bulging,—that one human being should be doing this for another. (p. 63)

Mabel feels sorry for Miss Milan, certainly; but she also feels a depth of warmth and intimacy with this woman (evidently of a lower social class than herself) which is utterly lacking in her interactions with her peers—'Miss Milan was much more real, much kinder' (p. 64). The authentic attention Miss Milan has paid to literally materializing Mabel's dress, the physical and mental effort she has expended on Mabel's fantasy of originality, is enough to bring tears to Mabel's eyes. This element of 'The New Dress' clearly gestures to an understanding of mutual affection between women whose lives might otherwise seem very different, but who are here brought close by the intimacy of one clothing the other's body.

A similar, if more intense, moment of intimacy between two women in a small room also features in ' "Slater's Pins Have No Points" ' which Woolf herself described as a 'nice little story about Sapphism',[24] although here the women bridge an age rather than class divide. This story does not, despite the hint of the title, feature a dressmaker, but rather a woman whose mere recognition that the material world exists is enough to give her younger admirer 'an extraordinary shock': 'Did Miss Craye actually go to Slater's and buy pins then, Fanny Wilmot asked herself, transfixed for a moment? [. . .] What need had she of pins? For she was not so much dressed as cased, like a beetle compact in its sheath, blue in winter, green in summer' (p. 69). To that point, Fanny has implicitly viewed her elegant, self-possessed piano teacher—a figure from another era who never married, whose family always had 'such lovely things' (p. 69)—as perhaps not possessing a body in need of clothing like other people: not being corporeal, not being sensual. This realization transforms Fanny's understanding of Julia Craye. Fanny looks up from the floor where she has been searching for the pin which has fallen off her dress—a pin that had fixed a rose to her breast—and from this position of prostration at the feet of her idol, her relationship with 'Julia' reaches an ambiguous but unmistakably erotic climax. The queerness (a term Woolf herself uses three times of Julia Craye) of this story is heightened by the fact that the titular object is one defined by not serving the purpose for which it is intended. A pin without a point is, presumably, not a pin at all—like the tablecloths alluded to in 'The Mark on the Wall' that were not 'real' tablecloths. The pin thus moves from being an object in the world with a clear purpose, whose efficient compliance with the purpose for which it was intended means it is very likely overlooked, to being a thing which not only draws attention to itself, but also becomes awkward, even uncanny. Specifically here it seems to provide an opportunity to imagine a world from a different angle: by extending the obvious phallic metaphor, a world without (pointless?) husbands, whom Julia Craye laughingly refers to as 'ogres'; or more literally, a world where a flower—part of a woman's dress whose vulnerability to falling from the body offers a clear hint at further disrobing—evades its usual role as a traditional heterosexual love-token. The flower which refuses to stay in its place is first described as a rose, but later as a carnation; whether this was an oversight on Woolf's part or not, the effect in this story is to further dislocate this object from its expected, clichéd function. Whatever kind of flower this rose/carnation is, it is certainly a queer one.

The narrator of 'The String Quartet' asks many explicit questions about the role of clothes and their relationship with the human psyche: 'if it's all the facts I mean, and the hats, the fur boas, the gentlemen's swallowtail coats, and pearl tie-pins that come to the surface—what chance is there?'; 'Why so anxious about the sit of cloaks; and gloves—whether to button or unbutton?' (pp. 38, 39). But these comments, which seem to dismiss clothing as superficial, even superfluous, are in stark contrast to a passage later in the story where we briefly dip into historical fiction. The music of the titular string quartet and its aftermath apparently evoke in the narrator a literally cloaked vision of sexual assault: the assailant 'trod on the lace of my petticoat', a sword then plays its all-too-familiar phallic role, as a woman is saved by a Prince 'in his velvet skull-cap, and furred slippers' whose rapier offers her a means of escape, ' "flinging on this cloak to hide the ravages to my skirt—to hide . . . But listen! the horns!" ' (p. 41). The stuttering repetition of 'hide', followed by the veiling of whatever is hidden by the ellipses, only draws attention to the sexual assault which the woman's clothing has apparently facilitated, or at least not enabled her easily to resist. Woolf may have been by turns fascinated and repelled by the role of fashion in society, but she was absolutely clear-sighted about how clothes, those physical objects we bear on our bodies at almost all times, have functioned historically to literally restrict women, to oppress them and weigh them down—a topic she would explore to the full, and with an extraordinary blend of humour and polemic, in her 1928 fantasy historical novel *Orlando*.

'And Truth?': Woolf's Questioning Ethics

The word 'object' does not, of course, just mean a physical thing. So when Woolf's narrator in 'The Mark on the Wall' reflects 'How readily our thoughts swarm upon a new object', we are asked both to imagine it literally, as something that a party of ants might pick up and move, and metaphorically, as a new idea, a new focus of attention; or indeed as an aim, an objective. The question of what fiction's object ought to be is central to one of Woolf's most famous essays, often read as a manifesto of sorts for her novelistic experimentation (although it is as much a description of the experimentation she saw already underway around her as a statement of her own intent). In this essay, originally published as 'Modern Novels' in 1919 and revised as 'Modern Fiction' in 1925, Woolf suggests that 'the proper stuff of fiction is a little other than custom would have us believe it', indeed later that ' "The proper stuff of fiction" does not exist, everything is the proper stuff of fiction, every feeling, every thought; every quality of brain and spirit is drawn upon; no perception comes amiss.'[25] Here, Woolf appears to be addressing the question of content: there should be no question of certain matters being excluded

from consideration by the fiction writer, nothing that lies beyond, or
beneath, their purview. 'Let us not take it for granted that life exists
more fully in what is commonly thought big than in what is commonly thought small',[26] Woolf suggests; and although this may well
be intended to summarize the approach Woolf detects in the work of
her contemporary James Joyce, her sympathy with this principle
seems vividly evident in the stories collected here. Indeed, despite the
fact that in both versions of this essay Woolf mainly discusses novelists, it is the Russian short story writer Anton Tchekhov (as Woolf
spelt it) whose work is mentioned most admiringly. In his story
'Gusev', Woolf observes:

The emphasis is laid on such unexpected places that at first it seems as if
there were no emphasis at all; and then, as the eyes accustom themselves to
twilight and discern the shapes of things in a room we see how complete the
story is, how profound [. . .] But it is impossible to say 'this is comic', or
'that is tragic', nor are we certain, since short stories, we have been taught,
should be brief and conclusive, whether this, which is vague and inconclusive, should be called a short story at all.[27]

The same could be—indeed has been—said about some of Woolf's
own multivalent, suggestive, even elusive short fictions; and Woolf
clearly admired what could be achieved in a few short pages.

The fundamental unknowability of other human beings is at the
heart of a number of Woolf's short fictions. The narrator of 'An
Unwritten Novel'—a well-developed character in her own right—
devises a complex inner and outer life for the woman sitting opposite
her in a train carriage, but finds her own world utterly upended when,
on departing the train, 'Minnie' (as the narrator has christened the
unnamed woman) proceeds into a life apparently utterly different
from that which the narrator has imagined for her: 'Well, my world's
done for! What do I stand on? What do I know? That's not Minnie.
There never was Moggridge. Who am I? Life's bare as bone' (p. 25).
'And yet', the narrator goes on, this feeling of utter confusion, ini-
tially struggling to realize the extent of her misapprehension, turns
not into resentment, anxiety, or fear, but into an ecstatic embrace of
the 'unknown figures' who surround us; their mystery, vigour, variety,
making up the 'adorable world' (p. 25). Paradoxically it is not forming

---

[26] 'Modern Fiction', 161.   [27] 'Modern Fiction', 162–3.

an accurate assessment of a stranger which makes for human connection, empathy, and compassion, but ultimately the recognition of her absolute otherness. And yet, of course, without the narrator's flight of imagination there would be no story; there would have been none of the pleasure of inventing a complex world for this person, their history, their family, the wider circles beyond them. Creating such a world itself relies on deep investment and interest in other human beings.

Woolf has in the past often been characterized as a bloodless writer, fighting shy of addressing the realities of material existence—particularly by comparison with, for example, James Joyce, whose explicit engagement with the bodily, and the taboos he broke in order to express it, led to the original publishers of his major work *Ulysses* (1922) being prosecuted under obscenity laws. But a more careful appraisal of Woolf's work reveals that she is, in fact, highly attuned to the bodily—and, in 'An Unwritten Novel', recognizes the somatic as a means of communication which goes beyond merely conveying an idea or emotion to another, but actually manifests itself in the sharing of a bodily experience. 'Minnie' has a physical tic, of scratching the small of her back in a manner which clearly nauseates the narrator: 'while she spoke she fidgeted as though the skin on her back were as a plucked fowl's in a poulterer's shop-window' (p. 17). But when 'Minnie' rubs at an apparent spot on the window, the narrator reports that 'something impelled me to take my glove and rub my window' in turn; and sure enough, what follows is that 'the spasm went through me; I crooked my arm and plucked at the middle of my back. My skin, too, felt like the damp chicken's skin in the poulterer's shop-window' (p. 18). In passing on this physical impulse, the narrator believes, 'she ["Minnie"] had communicated, shared her secret, passed her poison; she would speak no more' (p. 18). Although it transpires that the life the narrator has devised for 'Minnie', including presumably this dark secret lying at its heart, bears no relation to reality, nevertheless this corporeal communication, this bodily empathy, did really happen. It reminds us that these two women, if nothing else, shared the experience we all have: of having bodies which sometimes disobey us; which cause discomfort, even pain; which are ultimately beyond our control.

'The Lady in the Looking-Glass: A Reflection' similarly cautions against making assumptions about others' lives, while revelling in the pleasure of so doing. The opening paragraphs take us to a space not unlike that of 'A Haunted House', where light and air animate an apparently empty room; the looking-glass, however, halts that movement: 'in the looking-glass things had ceased to breathe and lay still in the trance of immortality' (p. 75), as if warning us that any attempt to represent, to reflect, can never capture life itself. Unlike in 'An Unwritten Novel', the protagonist of 'The Lady in the Looking-Glass' is well known to the narrator—the story may have been prompted by Woolf observing her friend the artist Ethel Sands 'not looking at her letters'[28]—and yet, 'after knowing her all these years one could not say what the truth about Isabella was' (p. 76). The end of the story appears to bring a reversal, in the manner of 'An Unwritten Novel' or indeed of 'The Mark on the Wall', where reality interrupts, and contradicts, the world that the story has created. Yet the conclusion of 'The Lady in the Looking-Glass' is not quite so clear. We leave Isabella, as she appears reflected in the looking-glass, in stark contrast to the passionate, vibrant woman described in the earlier pages: 'naked [. . .] empty [. . .] She had no thoughts. She had no friends. She cared for nobody' (p. 79). Yet the language leaves open the possibility that this, too, is an inaccurate understanding of Isabella: in particular, Woolf's repeated use of the word 'seemed' to introduce this scene. The supposed 'woman herself' we are left seeing, at the end of the story, may well only be another effect of the looking-glass—which, as we have seen, tends to render the animate inert, to petrify what is vibrant.

A key ethical aspect of Woolf's short fiction is, then, its dual insistence that the search for truth is both worthwhile and endless. It proposes 'truth' as something which we might legitimately seek— something which, in short, exists—while recognizing that this search is fraught with pitfalls, not least since there are self-appointed arbiters of what constitutes truth to contend with along the way. This is most apparent in 'A Society', a story which offers direct moments of social commentary (allusions to levels of hunger, incarceration, deaths in childbirth, as well as 'our rule in India, Africa and Ireland' (p. 49)—Jill even goes so far as to ask Sir Harley Tightboots about 'the capitalist system', no less (p. 50)), but which makes the reader constantly aware of the filter through which the answers to the young women's

[28] *Diary*, iii. 157.

questions are put. Statistics about social ills are valuable, the story suggests, but as Castalia's exasperated commentary implies, their provenance must be interrogated: 'All this time we have been talking of aeroplanes, factories and money. Let us talk about men themselves and their arts, for that is the heart of the matter' (p. 49). And it is, of course, almost exclusively men who have both provided those statistics (in answer to enquiries men have framed), and generated the conditions they describe. If supposedly hard facts do not provide adequate answers, then perhaps fiction will do so. Elizabeth, however, having spent five years disguised as a man in order to pass as a literary reviewer, comes to the conclusion that ' "the truth has nothing to do with literature" ' (p. 51)—which would appear a fairly self-defeating conclusion to come to in a short fiction, were it not that the literature she has been reviewing is that of the male realist novelists whose work Woolf most disdained.[29] Indeed, the problem with these writers, as Woolf saw it and as 'A Society' indicates, is that they appear too certain as to what truth is, what reality is (bolstered of course by their position of great privilege as white middle- or upper-class men), and see their role simply to reflect that truth and reality in their work. Woolf's approach is much less certain, and much more open.

It is as much in their formal features as their content that Woolf's short fictions set out their ethics: their commitment to truth-seeking alongside their scepticism about truth-finding. 'Monday or Tuesday' is one of the collection's more fragmentary, abstract pieces—like 'Blue & Green', closer to a prose poem than a conventional short story. Its four paragraphs, plus a single final line, are visually marked by numerous dashes, again drawing attention to the materiality of the text on the page, its existence in a visual as well as linguistic form, and also providing emphatic, if irregular, rhythmic punctuation. The other striking formal feature of this work is its refrain: 'desiring truth', repeated twice; and then 'truth?', repeated three times. The desire for truth, then, leads to framing the term as, emphatically, a question. This gesture of ethical questioning is found in a different form in 'In the Orchard', in its overall structure which presents what is apparently the same moment in three different ways: a young woman dozes—or seems to doze—over her book, lying beneath an

---

[29] See Explanatory Notes, note to p. 51.

apple tree in an orchard, until she suddenly realizes that she will be 'late for tea' (pp. 55–7). The first version focuses on spatial elements, as the narrative perspective moves higher and higher, from the apples 'Four feet in the air over her head' to 'the very topmost leaves of the apple tree [. . .] thirty feet above the earth' to the church spire 'two hundred feet above Miranda' and finally the wind, 'miles above Miranda lying in the orchard asleep' (p. 55). Sound is the key sensory connection here: the din of children repeating their times table, a 'solitary cry' of a drunken man, the church bells, and then the wind itself. In the second version, we are also given access to Miranda's thoughts, or perhaps dreams, and the narrative perspective moves around in space and time accordingly; indeed everything around her 'seemed driven out, round, and across by the beat of her own heart' (p. 56). The final section resembles a verbal still life; intensely visual, deeply attentive to the detail of the natural world around Miranda, with a narrative perspective and technique comparable to that Woolf employed a few years previously in 'Kew Gardens'. So which of these three versions, the piece implicitly asks us, tells the truth of this scene? The only possible answer, of course, is that they all do, and that there is in principle no limit to the truths that might be told about this moment, or the way in which they might be told. But the fact that each piece concludes with Miranda's realizing she will be late for tea—what might seem a banal punctuation of these intensely wrought, deeply concentrated pieces—has the effect of reminding us of the most basic of human needs: that we all must eat, and probably eat with others; that we have social networks that rely on us presenting ourselves at certain places and at certain times.

As the narrator of 'The Mark on the Wall' puts it:

As we face each other in omnibuses and underground railways we are looking into the mirror; that accounts for the vagueness, the gleam of glassiness, in our eyes. And the novelists in future will realize more and more the importance of these reflections, for of course there is not one reflection but an almost infinite number (p. 5)

Multiplicity is a key aesthetic and ethical principle of Woolf's work, vividly displayed in this collection of her short fiction. There are, however, limitations and shortcomings in their empathetic reach. Despite the power of her work's structural gesture towards acceptance and openness, the fact is that—for example—Woolf rarely provides sustained engagement with the interior lives of those from lower social classes than herself; indeed, some of her depictions of working-class people are, bluntly, patronizing, such as when the narrator of 'Kew Gardens' observes of the two 'women of the lower middle class [. . .] Like most people of their station they were frankly fascinated by any signs of eccentricity betokening a disordered brain, especially in the well-to-do' (p. 13). Woolf appeared well aware of the tone of this scene, recording in her diary that she was reluctant to show the story to members of the Women's Co-operative Guild, a women's political organization with which she was for a time involved and whose members came from all classes: 'I don't want them to read the scene of the two women. Is that to the discredit of Kew Gardens? Perhaps a little.'[30]

While Woolf did appear to make more of an effort to explore working-class voices during the early 1930s, as recent discoveries of unfinished short stories indicate,[31] and while she was highly sympathetic to political movements in support of the working classes, her own work tends to focus on the social strata with which she was most familiar. So while her attempts to articulate the experience of those from different social classes were limited, the gesture is discernible here and there. The same gesture in relation to racial difference is, however, barely present at all in her work. Urmila Seshagiri's observation that 'Woolf's interests in the concept of race are nowhere as explicit or well-developed as her interests in gender, war, class, or education'[32] is borne out by her short fiction, which offers little clear articulation of the significance of race as an aspect of human experience. The most direct mention of racial otherness found in this collection is, indeed, troubling, where Woolf uses the word 'nigger' (p. 20) to describe a Black man—or her narrator imagines the term being used casually in this way. It is true that the word was frequently used at the time by white people across public and private discourse

---

[30] *Diary*, i. 284.

[31] See Clara Jones, 'Virginia Woolf's 1931 "Cook Sketch"', *Woolf Studies Annual*, 20 (2014), 1–23; Susan Dick, 'Virginia Woolf's "The Cook"', *Woolf Studies Annual*, 3 (1997), 122–42.

[32] Urmila Seshagiri, *Race and the Modernist Imagination* (Ithaca, NY: Cornell University Press, 2010), 141. For key discussions of Woolf and race, see Seshagiri, *Race*, 140–91, and Jane Marcus, *Hearts of Darkness: White Women Write Race* (New Brunswick, NJ: Rutgers University Press, 2004), 24–58.

without censure or disquiet—with the apparent intention of providing a neutral description; a reflection, of course, of the profound and
systemic racism of the society in which Woolf lived.[33] But its use cannot simply be justified by saying that the term was not at the time
used in a derogatory way, since it certainly was; or by observing that
the word is here not Woolf's own but that of the narrator's imagined
woman, 'Minnie'. Likewise, noting that Woolf was a fervent critic of
the British Empire, and (largely through Leonard) involved in anti-
imperialist politics, does not neutralize the sting of the word—particularly when the context in which it is used seems to imply that the
man in question is one in a series of peculiarities or entertainments
one might encounter during the course of a stroll along the seafront.

The most fundamental ethical gesture of Woolf's work consists of its
attempt—flawed and partial though it may be—authentically to
understand what makes people what they are and how human lives are
intertwined, and continuing to attempt such a thing in the face of the
unknowability of others. The short story provides a 'space of encounter'—a structure which Christine Reynier has argued characterizes
all of Woolf's short fiction, and which Reynier describes as enabling
a kind of conversation which 'becomes indistinguishable from love or
sympathy or any other generous disposition where the self accommo-
dates the other without assimilating it but rather, respects its differences'.[34] This encounter can take place, Reynier suggests, on two
levels: the encounter is between self and other 'whether these are
defined as characters [. . .] or as writer and reader'.[35] That is to say,
some stories—such as 'An Unwritten Novel', 'The Lady in the
Looking-Glass', or indeed 'The New Dress'—clearly dramatize
encounters between particular characters, and explore the extent of,
and limits to, human understanding. But many of Woolf's stories
require the reader to encounter the text as an 'other', whose meanings
are multiple, even elusive. Refusing to provide a clear denouement
may not be to the taste of readers in search of simple answers and pat
conclusions in their fiction. An inconclusive story, even one whose

---

[33] For a full discussion of the history of this term, see Randall Kennedy, *Nigger: The
Strange Career of a Troublesome Word* (New York: Pantheon, 2002).

[34] Christine Reynier, *Virginia Woolf's Ethics of the Short Story* (London and
Basingstoke: Palgrave Macmillan, 2009), 70.

[35] Reynier, *Virginia Woolf's Ethics*, 17.

aesthetics is pleasing, may also leave the reader morally challenged. Do we admire and sympathize with the eccentric, or laugh at them? How much can we discover about our world through asking questions of those who govern that world? Which matter more: humans or snails? It is, of course, the very fact that the stories provide—indeed, constitute—questions rather than answers, that forms the basis of their ethical force. In both their subject matter—their capacity for empathy across a wide range of human experience—and their poetic features, these texts remind the reader of their own responsibility as active participant in the unfolding of stories about what it means to be human in this imperfect yet sometimes 'adorable world'.

NOTE ON THE TEXT

THESE stories appear in this collection in the order in which they were first published, reflecting the developments and changes in Woolf's experimentation with the short form over this period. All texts reprinted here are of the first published version of each story, with the exception of 'The Mark on the Wall', 'Kew Gardens', and 'An Unwritten Novel', which appear in the versions reprinted in *Monday or Tuesday* (abbreviated to *MT*; see the Appendix for details of variants between these first published versions and those in *MT*).

'The Mark on the Wall' was first published in July 1917 in *Two Stories* (see Introduction, pp. xii, xv), reprinted in 1919, and revised for inclusion in *MT*; 'Kew Gardens' was first published on 12 May 1919, reprinted in June of that year, and then reprinted in *MT*; 'An Unwritten Novel' was first published in the *London Mercury* (July 1920) and slightly revised for inclusion in *MT*; 'A Haunted House' was first published in *MT*; 'Monday or Tuesday' was first published in *MT*; 'Blue & Green' was first published in *MT*; 'The String Quartet' was first published in *MT*; 'A Society' was first published in *MT*; 'Solid Objects' first appeared in *The Athenaeum*, 4721 (22 October 1920), 543–5, and this is the text reprinted; 'In the Orchard' was first published in *The Criterion*, 1/3 (April 1923), 243–5, and this is the text reprinted; 'A Woman's College from Outside' first appeared in *Atalanta's Garland: being the book of the Edinburgh University Women's Union* (Edinburgh University Press, 1926), 11–16, and this is the text reprinted here; 'The New Dress' was first published in *Forum*, 77 (May 1927), 704–11, and this is the text reprinted; 'Slater's Pins have No Points' first appeared in *Forum*, 79 (January 1928), 58–63, and this is the text reprinted; 'The Lady in the Looking-Glass: A Reflection' was first published in *Harper's Magazine*, 160 (December 1929), 46–9 in the version reprinted here.

NOTE ON PUNCTUATION AND SPELLING

PUNCTUATION of the original texts has only been amended in this edition to correct clear errors (e.g. where a full stop is missing); by regularizing all ellipses to three dots; by removing all points after Mr, Mrs, etc; and by regularizing all speech marks to single inverted commas. We have also standardized ise/ize endings to ize.

Three of these stories—'The New Dress', '"Slater's Pins Have No Points"', and 'The Lady in the Looking-Glass'—were first published in the United States. However, North American spellings have been changed to British in this edition for consistency:

In 'The New Dress': 'clamor' becomes 'clamour' (p. 65).

In '"Slater's Pins Have No Points"': 'favor' becomes 'favour' (p. 69); 'checks' becomes 'cheques' (pp. 58 and 69); 'favorite' becomes 'favourite' (pp. 70 and 73); 'indorsing' becomes 'endorsing' (p. 70); 'water-colored' becomes 'water-coloured' (p. 71); 'savor' becomes 'savour' (p. 73); 'traveling' becomes 'travelling' (p. 74).

In 'The Lady in the Looking-Glass: A Reflection': 'check' becomes 'cheque' (p. 75); 'traveler's' becomes 'traveller's' (pp. 76 and 78); 'traveled' becomes 'travelled' (p. 78); 'color' becomes 'colour' (p. 77); 'molder' becomes 'moulder' (p. 78).

SELECT BIBLIOGRAPHY

Bibliography

Kirkpatrick, B. J., and Clarke, Stuart N., *A Bibliography of Virginia Woolf* (4th edn; Oxford: Clarendon Press, 1997).

Biography

Bell, Quentin, *Virginia Woolf: A Biography* (1972–3; London: Pimlico, 1996).
Briggs, Julia, *Virginia Woolf: An Inner Life* (London: Penguin, 2005).
Gordon, Lyndall, *Virginia Woolf: A Writer's Life* (Oxford: Oxford University Press, 1984).
Harris, Alexandra, *Virginia Woolf* (London: Thames & Hudson, 2011).
Leaska, Mitchell A., *Granite and Rainbow: The Hidden Life of Virginia Woolf* (London: Picador, 1998).
Lee, Hermione, *Virginia Woolf* (London: Chatto & Windus, 1996).
Mepham, John, *Virginia Woolf: A Literary Life* (London and Basingstoke: Macmillan, 1991).
Woolf, Leonard, *An Autobiography* (2 vols; Oxford: Oxford University Press, 1980).
Wright, Elizabeth, *Brief Lives: Virginia Woolf* (London: Hesperus Press, 2011).

Editions

The Complete Shorter Fiction of Virginia Woolf, ed. Susan Dick (1985; London: Hogarth Press, rev. edn 1989).
The Diary of Virginia Woolf, ed. Anne Olivier Bell and Andrew McNeillie (5 vols; London: Hogarth Press, 1977–84).
The Essays of Virginia Woolf, ed. Andrew McNeillie and Stuart N. Clarke (6 vols; London: Hogarth Press, 1986–2011).
Letters of Leonard Woolf, ed. Frederic Spotts (London: Weidenfeld & Nicolson, 1989).
The Letters of Virginia Woolf, ed. Nigel Nicolson and Joanne Trautmann (6 vols; London: Hogarth Press, 1975–80).
A Passionate Apprentice: The Early Journals 1897–1909, ed. Mitchell A. Leaska (London: Hogarth Press, 1990).

General Criticism

Abel, Elizabeth, *Virginia Woolf and the Fictions of Psychoanalysis* (Chicago: University of Chicago Press, 1989).
Allen, Judith, *Virginia Woolf and the Politics of Language* (Edinburgh: Edinburgh University Press, 2012).
Alt, Christina, *Virginia Woolf and the Study of Nature* (New York: Cambridge University Press, 2010).

Beer, Gillian, *Virginia Woolf: The Common Ground* (Edinburgh: Edinburgh University Press, 1996).

Berman, Jessica, *A Companion to Virginia Woolf* (Hoboken and Chichester: Wiley-Blackwell, 2016).

Bowlby, Rachel (ed.), *Virginia Woolf*, Longman Critical Readers series (London: Longman, 1992).

Bowlby, Rachel (ed.), *Virginia Woolf: Feminist Destinations and Further Essays on Virginia Woolf* (Edinburgh: Edinburgh University Press, 1997).

Briggs, Julia, *Reading Virginia Woolf* (Edinburgh: Edinburgh University Press, 2006).

Cuddy-Keane, Melba, *Virginia Woolf, the Intellectual, and the Public Sphere* (Cambridge: Cambridge University Press, 2003).

Detloff, Madelyn, *The Value of Virginia Woolf* (Cambridge: Cambridge University Press, 2016).

DiBattista, Maria, *Imagining Virginia Woolf: An Experiment in Critical Biography* (Princeton: Princeton University Press, 2009).

Dubino, Jeanne, *Virginia Woolf and the Literary Marketplace* (New York: Palgrave Macmillan, 2010).

Dubino, Jeanne, Lowe, Gill, Neverow, Vara, and Simpson, Kathryn (eds), *Virginia Woolf: Twenty-First Century Approaches* (Edinburgh: Edinburgh University Press, 2014).

Gillespie, Diane Filby, *The Sisters' Arts: The Writing and Painting of Virginia Woolf and Vanessa Bell* (Syracuse, NY: Syracuse University Press, 1988).

Goldman, Jane, *The Feminist Aesthetics of Virginia Woolf: Modernism, Post-Impressionism and the Politics of the Visual* (Cambridge: Cambridge University Press, 1998).

Humm, Maggie, *Snapshots of Bloomsbury: The Private Lives of Virginia Woolf and Vanessa Bell* (New Brunswick, NJ: Rutgers University Press, 2006).

Humm, Maggie (ed.), *The Edinburgh Companion to Virginia Woolf and the Arts* (Edinburgh: Edinburgh University Press, 2010).

Hussey, Mark, *Virginia Woolf A to Z: A Comprehensive Reference for Students, Teachers and Common Readers to her Life, Work and Critical Reception* (New York: Facts on File Inc., 1995).

Hussey, Mark (ed.), *Virginia Woolf and War: Fiction, Reality, and Myth* (Syracuse, NY: Syracuse University Press, 1991).

Jones, Clara, *Virginia Woolf: Ambivalent Activist* (Edinburgh: Edinburgh University Press, 2015).

Koppen, Randi, *Virginia Woolf: Fashion and Literary Modernity* (Edinburgh: Edinburgh University Press, 2009).

Laurence, Patricia Ondek, *The Reading of Silence: Virginia Woolf in the English Tradition* (Stanford, CA: Stanford University Press, 1991).

Light, Alison, *Mrs Woolf and the Servants* (London: Fig Tree, 2007).

Majumdar, Robin, and McLaurin, Allen (eds), *Virginia Woolf: The Critical Heritage* (1975; London: Routledge, 1997).

Marcus, Jane, *Virginia Woolf and the Languages of Patriarchy* (Bloomington, IN: Indiana University Press, 1987).

Marcus, Jane (ed.), *New Feminist Essays on Virginia Woolf* (Lincoln, NE: University of Nebraska Press, 1981).

Marcus, Laura, *Virginia Woolf*, Writers and Their Work series (1997; Liverpool: Liverpool University Press, 2004).

Naremore, James, *The World Without a Self: Virginia Woolf and the Novel* (New Haven: Yale University Press, 1973).

Phillips, Kathy J., *Virginia Woolf Against Empire* (Knoxville: University of Tennessee Press, 1994).

Randall, Bryony, and Goldman, Jane (eds), *Virginia Woolf in Context* (Cambridge: Cambridge University Press, 2013).

Roe, Sue, and Sellers, Susan (eds), *The Cambridge Companion to Virginia Woolf* (2000; Cambridge: Cambridge University Press, 2010).

Ryan, Derek, *Virginia Woolf and the Materiality of Theory: Sex, Animal, Life* (Edinburgh: Edinburgh University Press, 2013).

Scott, Bonnie Kime, *In the Hollow of the Wave: Virginia Woolf and Modernist Uses of Nature* (Charlottesville: University of Virginia Press, 2012).

Sim, Lorraine, *Virginia Woolf: The Patterns of Ordinary Experience* (Farnham: Ashgate, 2010).

Simpson, Kathryn, *Gifts, Markets and Economies of Desire in Virginia Woolf* (New York: Palgrave Macmillan, 2008).

Simpson, Kathryn, *Woolf: A Guide for the Perplexed* (London: Bloomsbury, 2016).

Snaith, Anna, *Virginia Woolf: Public and Private Negotiations* (London and Basingstoke: Macmillan, 2000).

Snaith, Anna (ed.), *Palgrave Advances in Virginia Woolf Studies* (London and Basingstoke: Palgrave Macmillan, 2007).

Southworth, Helen (ed.), *Leonard and Virginia Woolf: The Hogarth Press and the Networks of Modernism* (Edinburgh: Edinburgh University Press, 2010).

Spalding, Frances, *Virginia Woolf: Art, Life and Vision* (London: National Portrait Gallery, 2014).

Zwerdling, Alex, *Virginia Woolf and the Real World* (Berkeley and Los Angeles: University of California Press, 1986).

Criticism of the Modernist Short Story and Woolf's Short Fiction

Baldwin, Dean R., *Virginia Woolf: A Study of the Short Fiction* (Boston: Twayne, 1989).

Bayley, John, *The Short Story: Henry James to Elizabeth Bowen* (Brighton: Harvester Press, 1988).

Benzel, Kathryn N., and Hoberman, Ruth (eds), *Trespassing Boundaries: Virginia Woolf's Short Fiction* (New York: Palgrave, 2004).

Drewery, Claire, *Modernist Short Fiction by Women: the Liminal in Katherine Mansfield, Dorothy Richardson, May Sinclair and Virginia Woolf* (Farnham: Ashgate, 2011).

Flora, Joseph M. (ed.), *The English Short Story 1880–1945: A Critical History* (Boston: Twayne, 1985).

Hanson, Clare, *Short Stories and Short Fictions, 1880–1980* (London and Basingstoke: Macmillan, 1985).

Hanson, Clare (ed.), *Re-reading the Short Story* (London and Basingstoke: Macmillan, 1989).

Head, Dominic, *The Modernist Short Story: A Study in Theory and Practice* (Cambridge: Cambridge University Press, 1992).

Hunter, Adrian, *The Cambridge Introduction to the Short Story in English* (Cambridge: Cambridge University Press, 2007).

Hunter, Adrian, and Delaney, Paul (eds), *The Edinburgh Companion to the Short Story in English* (Edinburgh: Edinburgh University Press, 2018).

Krüger, Kate, *British Women Writers and the Short Story, 1850–1930: Reclaiming Social Space* (London: Palgrave Macmillan, 2014).

Levy, Heather, *The Servants of Desire in Virginia Woolf's Shorter Fiction* (New York: Peter Lang, 2010).

Liggins, Emma, Maunder, Andrew, and Robbins, Ruth, *The British Short Story* (New York: Palgrave Macmillan, 2011).

Malcolm, David, *The British and Irish Short Story Handbook* (Oxford: Wiley-Blackwell, 2012).

Reynier, Christine, *Virginia Woolf's Ethics of the Short Story* (London and Basingstoke: Palgrave Macmillan, 2009).

Reynier, Christine (ed.), *Journal of the Short Story in English*, 50 (Spring 2008) (special issue on Virginia Woolf).

Shaw, Valerie, *The Short Story: A Critical Introduction* (London: Longman, 1983).

Skrbic, Nena, *Wild Outbursts of Freedom: Reading Virginia Woolf's Short Fiction* (Westport, CT and London: Praeger, 2004).

Further Reading in Oxford World's Classics

Joyce, James, *Dubliners*, ed. Jeri Johnson.

Mansfield, Katherine, *Selected Stories*, ed. Dan Davin.

Whitworth, Michael, *Authors in Context: Virginia Woolf*.

Woolf, Virginia, *Between the Acts*, ed. Frank Kermode.

Woolf, Virginia, *Flush*, ed. Kate Flint.

Woolf, Virginia, *Jacob's Room*, ed. Kate Flint.

Woolf, Virginia, *Mrs Dalloway*, ed. David Bradshaw.

Woolf, Virginia, *Night and Day*, ed. Suzanne Raitt.

Woolf, Virginia, *Orlando: A Biography*, ed. Michael H. Whitworth.

Woolf, Virginia, *A Room of One's Own* and *Three Guineas*, ed. Anna Snaith.

Woolf, Virginia, *Selected Essays*, ed. David Bradshaw.

Woolf, Virginia, *To the Lighthouse*, ed. David Bradshaw.

Woolf, Virginia, *The Voyage Out*, ed. Lorna Sage.

Woolf, Virginia, *The Waves*, ed. David Bradshaw.

Woolf, Virginia, *The Years*, ed. Hermione Lee, with notes by Sue Ashbee.

A CHRONOLOGY OF VIRGINIA WOOLF

Life	*Historical and Cultural Background*
1882 (25 Jan.) Adeline Virginia Stephen (VW) born at 22 Hyde Park Gate, London.	Deaths of Darwin, Trollope, D. G. Rossetti; Joyce born; Stravinsky born; Married Women's Property Act; Society for Psychical Research founded.
1895 (5 May) Death of mother, Julia Stephen; VW's first breakdown occurs soon afterwards.	Death of T. H. Huxley; X-rays discovered; invention of the cinematograph; wireless telegraphy invented; arrest, trials, and conviction of Oscar Wilde. Wilde, *The Importance of Being Earnest* and *An Ideal Husband* Wells, *The Time Machine*
1896 (Nov.) Travels in France with sister Vanessa.	Death of William Morris; *Daily Mail* started. Hardy, *Jude the Obscure* Housman, *A Shropshire Lad*
1897 (10 April) Marriage of half-sister Stella; (19 July) death of Stella; (Nov.) VW learning Greek and History at King's College, London.	Queen Victoria's Diamond Jubilee; Tate Gallery opens. Stoker, *Dracula* James, *What Maisie Knew*
1898	Deaths of Gladstone and Lewis Carroll; radium and plutonium discovered. Wells, *The War of the Worlds*
1899 (30 Oct.) VW's brother Thoby goes up to Trinity College, Cambridge, where he forms friendships with Lytton Strachey, Leonard Woolf, Clive Bell, and others of the future Bloomsbury Group (VW's younger brother Adrian follows him to Trinity in 1902).	Boer War begins. Births of Bowen and Coward. Symons, *The Symbolist Movement in Literature* James, *The Awkward Age* Freud, *The Interpretation of Dreams*
1900	Deaths of Nietzsche, Wilde, and Ruskin; *Daily Express* started; Planck announces quantum theory; Boxer Rising. Conrad, *Lord Jim*

Life	*Historical and Cultural Background*
1901	Death of Queen Victoria; accession of Edward VII; first wireless communication between Europe and USA; 'World's Classics' series begun. Kipling, *Kim*
1902 VW starts private lessons in Greek with Janet Case.	End of Boer War; British Academy founded; *Encyclopaedia Britannica* (10th edn); *TLS* started. Bennett, *Anna of the Five Towns* James, *The Wings of the Dove*
1903	Deaths of Gissing and Spencer; *Daily Mirror* started; Wright brothers make their first aeroplane flight; Emmeline Pankhurst founds Women's Social and Political Union. Butler, *The Way of All Flesh* James, *The Ambassadors* Moore, *Principia Ethica*
1904 (22 Feb.) Death of father, Sir Leslie Stephen. In spring, VW travels to Italy with Vanessa and friend Violet Dickinson. (10 May) VW has second nervous breakdown and is ill for three months. Moves to 46 Gordon Square. (14 Dec.) VW's first publication appears.	Deaths of Christina Rossetti and Chekhov; Russo–Japanese War; *Entente Cordiale* between Britain and France. Chesterton, *The Napoleon of Notting Hill* Conrad, *Nostromo* James, *The Golden Bowl*
1905 (March, April) Travels in Portugal and Spain. Writes reviews and teaches once a week at Morley College, London.	Einstein, *Special Theory of Relativity*; Sartre born. Shaw, *Major Barbara* and *Man and Superman* Wells, *Kipps* Forster, *Where Angels Fear to Tread*
1906 (Sept. and Oct.) Travels in Greece. (20 Nov.) Death of Thoby Stephen.	Death of Ibsen; Beckett born; Liberal Government elected; Campbell-Bannerman Prime Minister; launch of HMS *Dreadnought*.
1907 (7 Feb.) Marriage of Vanessa to Clive Bell. VW moves with Adrian to 29 Fitzroy Square. At work on her first novel, 'Melymbrosia' (working title for *The Voyage Out*).	Auden born; Anglo-Russian Entente. Synge, *The Playboy of the Western World* Conrad, *The Secret Agent* Forster, *The Longest Journey*
1908 (Sept.) Visits Italy with the Bells.	Asquith Prime Minister; Old Age Pensions Act; Elgar's First Symphony. Bennett, *The Old Wives' Tale* Forster, *A Room with a View* Chesterton, *The Man Who Was Thursday*

Life	_Historical and Cultural Background_
1909 (17 Feb.) Lytton Strachey proposes marriage. (30 March) First meets Lady Ottoline Morrell. (April) Visits Florence. (Aug.) Visits Bayreuth and Dresden.	Death of Meredith; 'People's Budget'; English Channel flown by Blériot. Wells, _Tono-Bungay_ Masterman, _The Condition of England_ Marinetti, _Futurist Manifesto_
1910 (Jan.) Works for women's suffrage. (June–Aug.) Spends time in a nursing home at Twickenham.	Deaths of Edward VII, Tolstoy, and Florence Nightingale; accession of George V; _Encyclopaedia Britannica_ (11th edn); Roger Fry's Post-Impressionist Exhibition. Bennett, _Clayhanger_ Forster, _Howard's End_ Yeats, _The Green Helmet_ Wells, _The History of Mr Polly_
1911 (April) Travels to Turkey, where Vanessa is ill. (Nov.) Moves to 38 Brunswick Square, sharing house with Adrian, John Maynard Keynes, Duncan Grant, and Leonard Woolf.	National Insurance Act; Suffragette riots. Conrad, _Under Western Eyes_ Wells, _The New Machiavelli_ Lawrence, _The White Peacock_
1912 Rents Asheham House. (Feb.) Spends some days in Twickenham nursing home. (10 Aug.) Marriage to Leonard Woolf. Honeymoon in Provence, Spain, and Italy. (Oct.) Moves to 13 Clifford's Inn, London.	Second Post-Impressionist Exhibition; Suffragettes active; strikes by dockers, coal-miners, and transport workers; Irish Home Rule Bill rejected by Lords; sinking of SS _Titanic_; death of Scott in the Antarctic; _Daily Herald_ started. English translations of Chekhov and Dostoevsky begin to appear.
1913 (March) MS of _The Voyage Out_ delivered to publisher. Unwell most of summer. (9 Sept.) Suicide attempt. Remains under care of nurses and husband for rest of year.	_New Statesman_ started; Suffragettes active. Lawrence, _Sons and Lovers_
1914 (16 Feb.) Last nurse leaves. Moves to Richmond, Surrey.	Irish Home Rule Bill passed by Parliament; First World War begins (4 Aug.); Dylan Thomas born. Lewis, _Blast_ Joyce, _Dubliners_ Yeats, _Responsibilities_ Hardy, _Satires of Circumstance_ Bell, _Art_

Life	Historical and Cultural Background
1915 Purchase of Hogarth House, Richmond. (26 March) *The Voyage Out* published. (April, May) Bout of violent madness; under care of nurses until November.	Death of Rupert Brooke; Einstein, *General Theory of Relativity*; Second Battle of Ypres; Dardanelles Campaign; sinking of SS *Lusitania*; air attacks on London. Ford, *The Good Soldier* Lawrence, *The Rainbow* Brooke, *1914 and Other Poems* Richardson, *Pointed Roofs*
1916 (17 Oct.) Lectures to Richmond branch of the Women's Co-operative Guild. Regular work for *TLS*.	Death of James; Lloyd George Prime Minister; First Battle of the Somme; Battle of Verdun; Gallipoli Campaign; Easter Rising in Dublin. Joyce, *Portrait of the Artist as a Young Man*
1917 (July) Hogarth Press commences publication with 'The Mark on the Wall' and a story by Leonard Woolf. VW begins work on *Night and Day*.	Death of Edward Thomas; Third Battle of Ypres (Passchendaele); T. E. Lawrence's campaigns in Arabia; USA enters the War; Revolution in Russia (Feb., Oct.); Balfour Declaration. Eliot, *Prufrock and Other Observations*
1918 Writes reviews and *Night and Day*; also sets type for the Hogarth Press. (15 Nov.) First meets T. S. Eliot.	Death of Owen; Second Battle of the Somme; final German offensive collapses; Armistice with Germany (11 Nov.); Franchise Act grants vote to women over 30; influenza pandemic kills millions. Lewis, *Tarr* Hopkins, *Poems* Strachey, *Eminent Victorians*
1919 (1 July) Purchase of Monk's House, Rodmell, Sussex. (20 Oct.) *Night and Day* published.	Treaty of Versailles; Alcock and Brown fly the Atlantic; National Socialists founded in Germany. Sinclair, *Mary Olivier* Shaw, *Heartbreak House*
1920 Works on journalism and *Jacob's Room*.	League of Nations established. Pound, *Hugh Selwyn Mauberley* Lawrence, *Women in Love* Eliot, *The Sacred Wood* Fry, *Vision and Design*
1921 (7 or 8 April) *Monday or Tuesday* published. Ill for summer months. (4 Nov.) Finishes *Jacob's Room*.	Irish Free State founded. Huxley, *Crome Yellow*

Life	*Historical and Cultural Background*
1922 (Jan. to May) Ill. (14 Dec.) First meets Vita Sackville-West. (24 Oct.) *Jacob's Room* published.	Bonar Law Prime Minister; Mussolini forms Fascist Government in Italy; death of Proust; *Encyclopaedia Britannica* (12th edn); *Criterion* founded; BBC founded; Irish Free State proclaimed. Eliot, *The Waste Land* Galsworthy, *The Forsyte Saga* Joyce, *Ulysses* Mansfield, *The Garden Party* Wittgenstein, *Tractatus Logico-Philosophicus*
1923 (March, April) Visits Spain. Works on 'The Hours', the first version of *Mrs Dalloway*.	Baldwin Prime Minister; BBC radio begins broadcasting (Nov.); death of K. Mansfield.
1924 Purchase of lease on 52 Tavistock Square, Bloomsbury. Gives lecture that becomes 'Mr Bennett and Mrs Brown'. (8 Oct.) Finishes *Mrs Dalloway*.	First (minority) Labour Government; Ramsay MacDonald Prime Minister; deaths of Lenin, Kafka, and Conrad. Ford, *Some Do Not* Forster, *A Passage to India* O'Casey, *Juno and the Paycock* Coward, *The Vortex*
1925 (23 April) *The Common Reader* published. (14 May) *Mrs Dalloway* published. Ill during summer.	Gerhardie, *The Polyglots* Ford, *No More Parades* Huxley, *Those Barren Leaves* Whitehead, *Science and the Modern World*
1926 (Jan.) Unwell with German measles. Writes *To the Lighthouse*.	General Strike (3–12 May); *Encyclopaedia Britannica* (13th edn); first television demonstration. Ford, *A Man Could Stand Up* Tawney, *Religion and the Rise of Capitalism*
1927 (March, April) Travels in France and Italy. (5 May) *To the Lighthouse* published. (5 Oct.) Begins *Orlando*.	Lindburgh flies solo across the Atlantic; first 'talkie' films.
1928 (11 Oct.) *Orlando* published. Delivers lectures at Cambridge on which she bases *A Room of One's Own*.	Death of Hardy; votes for women over 21. Yeats, *The Tower* Lawrence, *Lady Chatterley's Lover* Waugh, *Decline and Fall* Sherriff, *Journey's End* Ford, *Last Post* Huxley, *Point Counter Point* Bell, *Civilization*

Life	*Historical and Cultural Background*
1929 (Jan.) Travels to Berlin. (24 Oct.) *A Room of One's Own* published.	2nd Labour Government, MacDonald Prime Minister; collapse of New York Stock Exchange; start of world economic depression. Graves, *Goodbye to All That* Aldington, *Death of a Hero* Green, *Living*
1930 (20 Feb.) First meets Ethel Smyth; (29 May) Finishes first version of *The Waves*.	Mass unemployment; television starts in USA; deaths of Lawrence and Conan Doyle. Auden, *Poems* Eliot, *Ash Wednesday* Waugh, *Vile Bodies* Coward, *Private Lives* Lewis, *Apes of God*
1931 (April) Car tour through France. (8 Oct.) *The Waves* published. Writes *Flush*.	Formation of National Government; abandonment of Gold Standard; death of Bennett; Japan invades China.
1932 (21 Jan.) Death of Lytton Strachey. (13 Oct.) *The Common Reader*, 2nd series, published. Begins *The Years*, at this point called 'The Pargiters'.	Roosevelt becomes President of USA; hunger marches start in Britain; *Scrutiny* starts. Huxley, *Brave New World*
1933 (May) Car tour of France and Italy. (5 Oct.) *Flush* published.	Deaths of Galsworthy and George Moore; Hitler becomes Chancellor of Germany. Orwell, *Down and Out in Paris and London* Wells, *The Shape of Things to Come*
1934 Works on *The Years*. (9 Sept.) Death of Roger Fry.	Waugh, *A Handful of Dust* Graves, *I, Claudius* Beckett, *More Pricks than Kicks* Toynbee, *A Study of History*
1935 Rewrites *The Years*. (May) Car tour of Holland, Germany, and Italy.	George V's Silver Jubilee; Baldwin Prime Minister of National Government; Germany re-arms; Italian invasion of Abyssinia (Ethiopia). Isherwood, *Mr Norris Changes Trains* T. S. Eliot, *Murder in the Cathedral*
1936 (May–Oct.) Ill. Finishes *The Years*. Begins *Three Guineas*.	Death of George V; accession of Edward VIII; abdication crisis; accession of George VI; Civil War breaks out in Spain; first of the Moscow show trials; Germany re-occupies the Rhineland; BBC television begins (2 Nov.); deaths of Chesterton, Kipling, and Housman. Orwell, *Keep the Aspidistra Flying*

Life	*Historical and Cultural Background*
1937 (15 March) *The Years* published. Begins *Roger Fry: A Biography*. (18 July) Death in Spanish Civil War of Julian Bell, son of Vanessa.	Chamberlain Prime Minister; destruction of Guernica; death of Barrie. Orwell, *The Road to Wigan Pier*
1938 (2 June) *Three Guineas* published. Works on *Roger Fry*, and begins to envisage *Between the Acts*.	German *Anschluss* with Austria; Munich agreement; dismemberment of Czechoslovakia; first jet engine. Beckett, *Murphy* Bowen, *The Death of the Heart* Greene, *Brighton Rock*
1939 VW moves to 37 Mecklenburgh Square, but lives mostly at Monk's House. Works on *Between the Acts*. Meets Freud in London.	End of Civil War in Spain; Russo-German pact; Germany invades Poland (Sept.); Britain and France declare war on Germany (3 Sept.); deaths of Freud, Yeats, and Ford. Joyce, *Finnegan's Wake* Isherwood, *Goodbye to Berlin*
1940 (25 July) *Roger Fry* published. (10 Sept.) Mecklenburgh Square house bombed. (18 Oct.) Witnesses the ruins of 52 Tavistock Square, destroyed by bombs. (23 Nov.) Finishes *Between the Acts*.	Germany invades north-west Europe; fall of France; evacuation of British troops from Dunkirk; Battle of Britain; beginning of 'the Blitz'; National Government under Churchill.
1941 (26 Feb.) Revises *Between the Acts*. Becomes ill. (28 March) Drowns herself in River Ouse, near Monk's House. (July) *Between the Acts* published.	Germany invades USSR; Japanese destroy US Fleet at Pearl Harbor; USA enters war; death of Joyce.

KEW GARDENS AND OTHER
SHORT FICTION

THE MARK ON THE WALL

PERHAPS it was the middle of January in the present year that I first looked up and saw the mark on the wall. In order to fix a date it is necessary to remember what one saw. So now I think of the fire; the steady film of yellow light upon the page of my book; the three chrysanthemums in the round glass bowl on the mantelpiece. Yes, it must have been the winter time, and we had just finished our tea, for I remember that I was smoking a cigarette when I looked up and saw the mark on the wall for the first time. I looked up through the smoke of my cigarette and my eye lodged for a moment upon the burning coals, and that old fancy of the crimson flag flapping from the castle tower came into my mind, and I thought of the cavalcade of red knights riding up the side of the black rock. Rather to my relief the sight of the mark interrupted the fancy, for it is an old fancy, an automatic fancy, made as a child perhaps. The mark was a small round mark, black upon the white wall, about six or seven inches above the mantelpiece.

How readily our thoughts swarm upon a new object, lifting it a little way, as ants carry a blade of straw so feverishly, and then leave it . . . If that mark was made by a nail, it can't have been for a picture, it must have been for a miniature—the miniature of a lady with white powdered curls, powder-dusted cheeks, and lips like red carnations.* A fraud of course, for the people who had this house before us would have chosen pictures in that way—an old picture for an old room. That is the sort of people they were—very interesting people, and I think of them so often, in such queer places, because one will never see them again, never know what happened next. They wanted to leave this house because they wanted to change their style of furniture, so he said, and he was in process of saying that in his opinion art should have ideas behind it when we were torn asunder, as one is torn from the old lady about to pour out tea and the young man about to hit the tennis ball in the back garden of the suburban villa as one rushes past in the train.

But as for that mark, I'm not sure about it; I don't believe it was made by a nail after all; it's too big, too round, for that. I might get up, but if I got up and looked at it, ten to one I shouldn't be able to say for certain; because once a thing's done, no one ever knows how it happened. O dear me, the mystery of life! The inaccuracy of thought! The ignorance of humanity! To show very little control of our possessions we have—what an accidental affair this living is after all our civilization—let me just count over a few of the things lost in one lifetime, beginning, for that seems always the most mysterious of losses—what cat would gnaw, what rat would nibble—three pale blue canisters of book-binding tools? Then there were the bird cages, the iron hoops, the steel skates, the Queen Anne coal-scuttle,* the bagatelle board,* the hand organ*—all gone, and jewels too. Opals and emeralds, they lie about the roots of turnips. What a scraping paring affair it is to be sure! The wonder is that I've any clothes on my back, that I sit surrounded by solid furniture at this moment. Why, if one wants to compare life to anything, one must liken it to being blown through the Tube* at fifty miles an hour landing at the other end without a single hairpin in one's hair! Shot out at the feet of God entirely naked! Tumbling head over heels in the asphodel meadows* like brown paper parcels pitched down a shoot in the post office! With one's hair flying back like the tail of a race-horse. Yes, that seems to express the rapidity of life, the perpetual waste and repair; all so casual, all so haphazard . . .

But after life. The slow pulling down of thick green stalks so that the cup of the flower, as it turns over, deluges one with purple and red light. Why, after all, should one not be born there as one is born here, helpless, speechless, unable to focus one's eyesight, groping at the roots of the grass, at the toes of the Giants? As for saying which are trees, and which are men and women, or whether there are such things, that one won't be in a condition to do for fifty years or so. There will be nothing but spaces of light and dark, intersected by thick stalks, and rather higher up perhaps, rose-shaped blots of an indistinct colour—dim pinks and blues—which will, as time goes on, become more definite, become—I don't know what . . .

And yet that mark on the wall is not a hole at all. It may even be caused by some round black substance, such as a small rose leaf, left over from the summer, and I, not being a very vigilant house-keeper—look at the dust on the mantelpiece, for example, the dust which, so they say, buried Troy three times over,* only fragments of pots utterly refusing annihilation, as one can believe.

The tree outside the window taps very gently on the pane . . . I want to think quietly, calmly, spaciously, never to be interrupted, never to have to rise from my chair, to slip easily from one thing to another, without any sense of hostility, or obstacle. I want to sink deeper and deeper, away from the surface, with its hard separate facts. To steady myself, let me catch hold of the first idea that passes . . . Shakespeare . . . Well, he will do as well as another. A man who sat himself solidly in an arm-chair, and looked into the fire, so— A shower of ideas fell perpetually from some very high Heaven down through his mind. He leant his forehead on his hand, and people, looking in through the open door,—for this scene is supposed to take place on a summer's evening,—But how dull this is, this historical fiction! It doesn't interest me at all. I wish I could hit upon a pleasant track of thought, a track indirectly reflecting credit upon myself, for those are the pleasantest thoughts, and very frequent even in the minds of modest mouse-coloured people, who believe genuinely that they dislike to hear their own praises. They are not thoughts directly praising oneself; that is the beauty of them; they are thoughts like this:

'And then I came into the room. They were discussing botany. I said how I'd seen a flower growing on a dust heap on the site of an old house in Kingsway.* The seed, I said, must have been sown in the reign of Charles the First.* What flowers grew in the reign of Charles the First?' I asked—(but I don't remember the answer). Tall flowers with purple tassels to them perhaps.* And so it goes on. All the time I'm dressing up the figure of myself in my own mind, lovingly, stealthily, not openly adoring it, for if I did that, I should catch myself out, and stretch my hand at once for a book in self-protection. Indeed, it is curious how instinctively one protects the image of oneself from idolatry or any other handling that could make it ridiculous, or too unlike the original to be believed in any longer. Or is it not so very curious after all? It is a matter of great importance. Suppose the looking-glass smashes, the image disappears, and the romantic figure with the green of forest depths all about it is there no longer, but only that shell of a person which is seen by other people—what an airless, shallow, bald, prominent world it becomes! A world not to be lived in. As we face each other in omnibuses and underground railways we are looking into the mirror; that accounts for the vagueness, the gleam of glassiness, in our eyes. And the novelists in future will realize more and more the importance of these reflections, for of course there is not one reflection but an almost infinite number; those are the depths they will explore, those the phantoms they will pursue, leaving the description of reality more and more out of their stories, taking a knowledge of it for granted, as the Greeks did and Shakespeare perhaps—but these generalizations are very worthless. The military sound of the word is enough. It recalls leading articles, cabinet ministers—a whole class of things indeed which as a child one thought the thing itself, the standard thing, the real thing, from which one could not depart save at the risk of nameless damnation. Generalizations bring back somehow Sunday in London, Sunday afternoon walks, Sunday luncheons, and also ways of speaking of the dead, clothes, and habits—like the habit of sitting all together in one room until a certain hour, although nobody liked it. There was a rule for everything. The rule for tablecloths at that particular period was that they should be made of tapestry with little yellow compartments marked upon them, such as you may see in photographs of the carpets in the corridors of the royal palaces. Tablecloths of a different kind were not real tablecloths. How shocking, and yet how wonderful it was to discover that these real things, Sunday luncheons, Sunday walks, country houses, and tablecloths were not entirely real, were indeed half phantoms, and the damnation which visited the disbeliever in them was only a sense of illegitimate freedom. What now takes the place of those things I wonder, those real standard things? Men perhaps, should you be a woman; the masculine point of view which governs our lives, which sets the standard, which establishes Whitaker's Table of Precedency,* which has become, I suppose, since the war half a phantom to many men and women, which soon, one may hope, will be laughed into the dustbin where the phantoms go, the mahogany sideboards and the Landseer prints,* Gods and Devils, Hell and so forth, leaving us all with an intoxicating sense of illegitimate freedom—if freedom exists . . .

In certain lights that mark on the wall seems actually to project from the wall. Nor is it entirely circular. I cannot be sure, but it seems to cast a perceptible shadow, suggesting that if I ran my finger down that strip of the wall it would, at a certain point, mount and descend a small tumulus, a smooth tumulus like those barrows on the South Downs which are, they say, either tombs or camps.* Of the two I should prefer them to be tombs, desiring melancholy like most English people, and finding it natural at the end of a walk to think of the bones stretched beneath the turf . . . There must be some book about it. Some antiquary must have dug up those bones and given them a name ... What sort of a man is an antiquary, I wonder? Retired Colonels for the most part, I daresay, leading parties of aged labourers to the top here, examining clods of earth and stone, and getting into correspondence with the neighbouring clergy, which, being opened at breakfast time, gives them a feeling of importance, and the comparison of arrow-heads necessitates cross-country journeys to the county towns, an agreeable necessity both to them and to their elderly wives, who wish to make plum jam or to clean out the study, and have every reason for keeping that great question of the camp or the tomb in perpetual suspension, while the Colonel himself feels agreeably philosophic in accumulating evidence on both sides of the question. It is true that he does finally incline to believe in the camp; and, being opposed, indites a pamphlet which he is about to read at the quarterly meeting of the local society when a stroke lays him low, and his last conscious thoughts are not of wife or child, but of the camp and that arrowhead there, which is now in the case at the local museum, together with the foot of a Chinese murderess, a handful of Elizabethan nails, a great many Tudor clay pipes, a piece of Roman pottery, and the wine-glass that Nelson drank out of—proving I really don't know what.

No, no, nothing is proved, nothing is known. And if I were to get up at this very moment and ascertain that the mark on the wall is really—what shall we say?—the head of a gigantic old nail, driven in two hundred years ago, which has now, owing to the patient attrition of many generations of housemaids, revealed its head above the coat of paint, and is taking its first view of modern life in the sight of a white-walled fire-lit room, what should I gain?—Knowledge? Matter for further speculation? I can think sitting still as well as standing up. And what is knowledge? What are our learned men save the descendants of witches and hermits who crouched in caves and in woods brewing herbs, interrogating shrew-mice and writing down the language of the stars? And the less we honour them as our superstitions dwindle and our respect for beauty and health of mind increases ... Yes, one could imagine a very pleasant world. A quiet spacious world, with the flowers so red and blue in the open fields. A world without professors or specialists or house-keepers with the profiles of policemen, a world which one could slice with one's thought as a fish slices the water with his fin, grazing the stems of the water-lilies, hanging suspended over nests of white sea eggs ... How peaceful it is down here, rooted in the centre of the world and gazing up through the gray waters, with their sudden gleams of light, and their reflections—If it were not for Whitaker's Almanack—if it were not for the Table of Precedency!

I must jump up and see for myself what that mark on the wall really is—a nail, a rose-leaf, a crack in the wood?

Here is Nature once more at her old game of self-preservation. This train of thought, she perceives, is threatening mere waste of energy, even some collision with reality, for who will ever be able to lift a finger against Whitaker's Table of Precedency? The Archbishop of Canterbury is followed by the Lord High Chancellor; the Lord High Chancellor is followed by the Archbishop of York. Everybody follows somebody, such is the philosophy of Whitaker; and the great thing is to know who follows whom. Whitaker knows, and let that, so Nature counsels, comfort you, instead of enraging you; and if you can't be comforted, if you must shatter this hour of peace, think of the mark on the wall.

I understand Nature's game—her prompting to take action as a way of ending any thought that threatens to excite or to pain. Hence, I suppose, comes our slight contempt for men of action—men, we assume, who don't think. Still, there's no harm in putting a full stop to one's disagreeable thoughts by looking at a mark on the wall.

Indeed, now that I have fixed my eyes upon it, I feel that I have grasped a plank in the sea; I feel a satisfying sense of reality which at once turns the two Archbishops and the Lord High Chancellor to the shadows of shades. Here is something definite, something real. Thus, waking from a midnight dream of horror, one hastily turns on the light and lies quiescent, worshipping the chest of drawers, worshipping solidity, worshipping reality, worshipping the impersonal world which is a proof of some existence other than ours. That is what one wants to be sure of . . . Wood is a pleasant thing to think about. It comes from a tree; and trees grow, and we don't know how they grow. For years and years they grow, without paying any attention to us, in meadows, in forests, and by the side of rivers—all things one likes to think about. The cows swish their tails beneath them on hot afternoons; they paint rivers so green that when a moorhen dives one expects to see its feathers all green when it comes up again. I like to think of the fish balanced against the stream like flags blown out; and of water-beetles slowly raising domes of mud upon the bed of the river. I like to think of the tree itself: first the close dry sensation of being wood; then the grinding of the storm; then the slow, delicious ooze of sap. I like to think of it, too, on winter's nights standing in the empty field with all leaves close-furled, nothing tender exposed to the iron bullets of the moon, a naked mast upon an earth that goes tumbling, tumbling, all night long. The song of birds must sound very loud and strange in June; and how cold the feet of insects must feel upon it, as they make laborious progresses up the creases of the bark, or sun themselves upon the thin green awning of the leaves, and look straight in front of them with diamond-cut red eyes . . . One by one the fibres snap beneath the immense cold pressure of the earth, then the last storm comes and, falling, the highest branches drive deep into the ground again. Even so, life isn't done with; there are a million patient, watchful lives still for a tree, all over the world, in bedrooms, in ships, on the pavement, lining rooms where men and women sit after tea, smoking cigarettes. It is full of peaceful thoughts, happy thoughts, this tree. I should like to take each one separately—but something is getting in the way . . . Where was I? What has it all been about? A tree? A river? The Downs? Whitaker's Almanack? The fields of asphodel? I can't remember a thing. Everything's moving, falling, slipping, vanishing . . . There is a vast upheaval of matter. Someone is standing over me and saying—

'I'm going out to buy a newspaper.'

'Yes?'

'Though it's no good buying newspapers . . . Nothing ever happens. Curse this war!* God damn this war! . . . All the same, I don't see why we should have a snail on our wall.'

Ah, the mark on the wall! It was a snail.

KEW GARDENS

FROM the oval shaped flower-bed there rose perhaps a hundred stalks spreading into heart shaped or tongue shaped leaves half way up and unfurling at the tip red or blue or yellow petals marked with spots of colour raised upon the surface; and from the red, blue or yellow gloom of the throat emerged a straight bar, rough with gold dust and slightly clubbed at the end.* The petals were voluminous enough to be stirred by the summer breeze, and when they moved, the red blue and yellow lights passed one over the other, staining an inch of the brown earth beneath with a spot of the most intricate colour. The light fell either upon the smooth grey back of a pebble, or the shell of a snail with its brown circular veins, or, falling into a raindrop, it expanded with such intensity of red, blue and yellow the thin walls of water that one expected them to burst and disappear. Instead, the drop was left in a second silver grey once more, and the light now settled upon the flesh of a leaf, revealing the branching thread of fibre beneath the surface, and again it moved on and spread its illumination in the vast green spaces beneath the dome of the heart shaped and tongue shaped leaves. Then the breeze stirred rather more briskly overhead and the colour was flashed into the air above, into the eyes of the men and women who walk in Kew Gardens in July.*

The figures of these men and women straggled past the flower-bed with a curiously irregular movement not unlike that of the white and blue butterflies who crossed the turf in zig-zag flights from bed to bed. The man was about six inches in front of the woman, strolling carelessly, while she bore on with greater purpose, only turning her head now and then to see that the children were not too far behind. The man kept this distance in front of the woman purposely, though perhaps unconsciously, for he wished to go on with his thoughts.

'Fifteen years ago I came here with Lily,'* he thought. 'We sat somewhere over there by a lake, and I begged her to marry me all through the hot afternoon. How the dragonfly kept circling round us: how clearly I see the dragonfly and her shoe with the square silver buckle at the toe. All the time I spoke I saw her shoe and when it moved impatiently I knew without looking up what she was going to say: the whole of her seemed to be in her shoe. And my love, my desire, were in the dragonfly; for some reason I thought that if it settled there, on that leaf, the broad one with the red flower in the middle of it, if the dragonfly settled on the leaf she would say "Yes" at once. But the dragonfly went round and round: it never settled anywhere—of course not, happily not, or I shouldn't be walking here with Eleanor and the children—Tell me, Eleanor. D'you ever think of the past?'

'Why do you ask, Simon?'

'Because I've been thinking of the past. I've been thinking of Lily, the woman I might have married . . . Well, why are you silent? Do you mind my thinking of the past?'

'Why should I mind, Simon? Doesn't one always think of the past, in a garden with men and women lying under the trees? Aren't they one's past, all that remains of it, those men and women, those ghosts lying under the trees, . . . one's happiness, one's reality?'

'For me, a square silver shoe buckle and a dragonfly—'

'For me, a kiss. Imagine six little girls sitting before their easels twenty years ago, down by the side of a lake, painting the water-lilies, the first red water-lilies I'd ever seen. And suddenly a kiss, there on the back of my neck. And my hand shook all the afternoon so that I couldn't paint. I took out my watch and marked the hour when I would allow myself to think of the kiss for five minutes only—it was so precious—the kiss of an old grey-haired woman with a wart on her nose, the mother of all my kisses all my life.* Come Caroline, come Hubert.'

They walked on past the flower-bed, now walking four abreast, and soon diminished in size among the trees and looked half transparent as the sunlight and shade swam over their backs in large trembling irregular patches.

In the oval flower bed the snail, whose shell had been stained red, blue, and yellow for the space of two minutes or so, now appeared to be moving very slightly in its shell, and next began to labour over the crumbs of loose earth which broke away and rolled down as it passed over them. It appeared to have a definite goal in front of it, differing in this respect from the singular high stepping angular green insect who attempted to cross in front of it, and waited for a second with its antennæ trembling as if in deliberation, and then stepped off as rapidly and strangely in the opposite direction. Brown cliffs with deep green lakes in the hollows, flat bladelike trees that waved from root to tip, round boulders of grey stone, vast crumpled surfaces of a thin crackling texture—all these objects lay across the snail's progress between one stalk and another to his goal. Before he had decided whether to circumvent the arched tent of a dead leaf or to breast it there came past the bed the feet of other human beings.

This time they were both men. The younger of the two wore an expression of perhaps unnatural calm; he raised his eyes and fixed them very steadily in front of him while his companion spoke, and directly his companion had done speaking he looked on the ground again and sometimes opened his lips only after a long pause and sometimes did not open them at all. The elder man had a curiously uneven and shaky method of walking, jerking his hand forward and throwing up his head abruptly, rather in the manner of an impatient carriage horse tired of waiting outside a house; but in the man these gestures were irresolute and pointless. He talked almost incessantly; he smiled to himself and again began to talk, as if the smile had been an answer. He was talking about spirits—the spirits of the dead, who, according to him, were even now telling him all sorts of odd things about their experiences in Heaven.

'Heaven was known to the ancients as Thessaly,* William, and now, with this war, the spirit matter is rolling between the hills like thunder.' He paused, seemed to listen, smiled, jerked his head and continued:—

'You have a small electric battery and a piece of rubber to insulate the wire—isolate?—insulate?—well, we'll skip the details, no good going into details that wouldn't be understood—and in short the little machine stands in any convenient position by the head of the bed, we will say, on a neat mahogany stand. All arrangements being properly fixed by workmen under my direction, the widow applies her ear and summons the spirit by sign as agreed. Women! Widows! Women in black—'

Here he seemed to have caught sight of a woman's dress in the distance, which in the shade looked a purple black. He took off his hat, placed his hand upon his heart, and hurried towards her muttering and gesticulating feverishly. But William caught him by the sleeve and touched a flower with the tip of his walking-stick in order to divert the old man's attention. After looking at it for a moment in some confusion the old man bent his ear to it and seemed to answer a voice speaking from it, for he began talking about the forests of

Uruguay which he had visited hundreds of years ago in company with the most beautiful young woman in Europe. He could be heard murmuring about forests of Uruguay blanketed with the wax petals of tropical roses, nightingales, sea beaches, mermaids, and women drowned at sea,* as he suffered himself to be moved on by William, upon whose face the look of stoical patience grew slowly deeper and deeper.

Following his steps so closely as to be slightly puzzled by his gestures came two elderly women of the lower middle class, one stout and ponderous, the other rosy cheeked and nimble. Like most people of their station they were frankly fascinated by any signs of eccentricity betokening a disordered brain, especially in the well-to-do; but they were too far off to be certain whether the gestures were merely eccentric or genuinely mad. After they had scrutinized the old man's back in silence for a moment and given each other a queer, sly look, they went on energetically piecing together their very complicated dialogue:

'Nell, Bert, Lot, Cess, Phil, Pa, he says, I says, she says, I says, I says, I says—'

'My Bert, Sis, Bill, Grandad, the old man, sugar,

> Sugar, flour, kippers, greens,
> Sugar, sugar, sugar.'

The ponderous woman looked through the pattern of falling words at the flowers standing cool, firm, and upright in the earth, with a curious expression. She saw them as a sleeper waking from a heavy sleep sees a brass candlestick reflecting the light in an unfamiliar way, and closes his eyes and opens them, and seeing the brass candlestick again, finally starts broad awake and stares at the candlestick with all his powers. So the heavy woman came to a standstill opposite the oval shaped flower bed, and ceased even to pretend to listen to what the other woman was saying. She stood there letting the words fall over her, swaying the top part of her body slowly backwards and forwards, looking at the flowers. Then she suggested that they should find a seat and have their tea.

The snail had now considered every possible method of reaching his goal without going round the dead leaf or climbing over it. Let alone the effort needed for climbing a leaf, he was doubtful whether the thin texture which vibrated with such an alarming crackle when touched even by the tip of his horns would bear his weight; and this determined him finally to creep beneath it, for there was a point where the leaf curved high enough from the ground to admit him. He had just inserted his head in the opening and was taking stock of the high brown roof and was getting used to the cool brown light when two other people came past outside on the turf. This time they were both young, a young man and a young woman. They were both in the prime of youth, or even in that season which precedes the prime of youth, the season before the smooth pink folds of the flower have burst their gummy case, when the wings of the butterfly, though fully grown, are motionless in the sun.

'Lucky it isn't Friday,' he observed.

'Why? D'you believe in luck?'

'They make you pay sixpence on Friday.'*

'What's sixpence anyway? Isn't it worth sixpence?'

'What's "it"—what do you mean by "it"?'

'O anything—I mean—you know what I mean.'

Long pauses came between each of these remarks; they were uttered in toneless and monotonous voices. The couple stood still on the edge of the flower bed, and together pressed the end of her parasol deep down into the soft earth. The action and the fact that his hand rested on the top of hers expressed their feelings in a strange way, as these short insignificant words also expressed something, words with short wings for their heavy body of meaning, inadequate to carry them far and thus alighting awkwardly upon the very common objects that surrounded them, and were to their inexperienced touch so massive; but who knows (so they thought as they pressed the parasol into the earth) what precipices aren't concealed in them, or what slopes of ice don't shine in the sun on the other side? Who knows? Who has ever seen this before? Even when she wondered what sort of tea they gave you at Kew,* he felt that something loomed up behind her words, and stood vast and solid behind them; and the mist very slowly rose and uncovered—O Heavens, what were those shapes?—little white tables, and waitresses who looked first at her and then at him; and there was a bill that he would pay with a real two shilling piece, and it was real, all real, he assured himself, fingering the coin in his pocket, real to everyone except to him and to her; even to him it began to seem real; and then—but it was too exciting to stand and think any longer, and he pulled the parasol out of the earth with a jerk and was impatient to find the place where one had tea with other people, like other people.

'Come along, Trissie; it's time we had our tea.'

'Wherever *does* one have one's tea?' she asked with the oddest thrill of excitement in her voice, looking vaguely round and letting herself be drawn on down the grass path, trailing her parasol, turning her head this way and that way, forgetting her tea, wishing to go down there and then down there, remembering orchids and cranes among wild flowers, a Chinese pagoda* and a crimson crested bird; but he bore her on.

Thus one couple after another with much the same irregular and aimless movement passed the flower-bed and were enveloped in layer after layer of green blue vapour, in which at first their bodies had substance and a dash of colour, but later both substance and colour dissolved in the green-blue atmosphere. How hot it was! So hot that even the thrush chose to hop, like a mechanical bird, in the shadow of the flowers, with long pauses between one movement and the next; instead of rambling vaguely the white butterflies danced one above another, making with their white shifting flakes the outline of a shattered marble column above the tallest flowers; the glass roofs of the palm house* shone as if a whole market full of shiny green umbrellas had opened in the sun; and in the drone of the aeroplane the voice of the summer sky murmured its fierce soul. Yellow and black, pink and snow white, shapes of all these colours, men, women, and children were spotted for a second upon the horizon, and then, seeing the breadth of yellow that lay upon the grass, they wavered and sought shade beneath the trees, dissolving like drops of water in the yellow and green atmosphere, staining it faintly with red and blue. It seemed as if all gross and heavy bodies had sunk down in the heat motionless and lay huddled upon the ground, but their voices went wavering from them as if they were flames lolling from the thick waxen bodies of candles. Voices. Yes, voices. Wordless voices, breaking the silence suddenly with such depth of contentment, such passion of desire, or, in the voices of children, such freshness of surprise; breaking the silence? But there was no silence; all the time the motor omnibuses were turning their wheels and changing their gear; like a vast nest of Chinese boxes* all of wrought steel turning ceaselessly one within another the city murmured; on the top of which the voices cried aloud and the petals of myriads of flowers flashed their colours into the air.

AN UNWRITTEN NOVEL

Such an expression of unhappiness was enough by itself to make one's eyes slide above the paper's edge to the poor woman's face—insignificant without that look, almost a symbol of human destiny with it. Life's what you see in people's eyes; life's what they learn, and, having learnt it, never, though they seek to hide it, cease to be aware of—what? That life's like that, it seems. Five faces opposite—five mature faces—and the knowledge in each face. Strange, though, how people want to conceal it! Marks of reticence are on all those faces: lips shut, eyes shaded, each one of the five doing something to hide or stultify his knowledge. One smokes; another reads; a third checks entries in a pocket book; a fourth stares at the map of the line framed opposite;* and the fifth—the terrible thing about the fifth is that she does nothing at all. She looks at life. Ah, but my poor, unfortunate woman, do play the game—do, for all our sakes, conceal it!

As if she heard me, she looked up, shifted slightly in her seat and sighed. She seemed to apologize and at the same time to say to me, 'If only you knew!' Then she looked at life again. 'But I do know,' I answered silently, glancing at the *Times* for manners' sake: 'I know the whole business. "Peace between Germany and the Allied Powers was yesterday officially ushered in at Paris—Signor Nitti, the Italian Prime Minister—a passenger train at Doncaster was in collision with a goods train . . ." We all know—the *Times* knows—but we pretend we don't.' My eyes had once more crept over the paper's rim. She shuddered, twitched her arm queerly to the middle of her back and shook her head. Again I dipped into my great reservoir of life. 'Take what you like,' I continued, 'births, deaths, marriages, Court Circular, the habits of birds, Leonardo da Vinci, the Sandhills murder, high wages and the cost of living—oh, take what you like,' I repeated, 'it's all in the *Times*!'* Again with infinite weariness she moved her head from side to side until, like a top exhausted with spinning, it settled on her neck.

The *Times* was no protection against such sorrow as hers. But other human beings forbade intercourse. The best thing to do against life was to fold the paper so that it made a perfect square, crisp, thick, impervious even to life. This done, I glanced up quickly, armed with a shield of my own. She pierced through my shield; she gazed into my eyes as if searching any sediment of courage at the depths of them and damping it to clay. Her twitch alone denied all hope, discounted all illusion.

So we rattled through Surrey and across the border into Sussex. But with my eyes upon life I did not see that the other travellers had left, one by one, till, save for the man who read, we were alone together. Here was Three Bridges station. We drew slowly down the platform and stopped. Was he going to leave us? I prayed both ways—I prayed last that he might stay. At that instant he roused himself, crumpled his paper contemptuously, like a thing done with, burst open the door and left us alone.

The unhappy woman, leaning a little forward, palely and colourlessly addressed me—talked of stations and holidays, of brothers at Eastbourne, and the time of year, which was, I forget now, early or late. But at last looking from the window and seeing, I knew, only life, she breathed, 'Staying away—that's the drawback of it——' Ah, now we approached the catastrophe, 'My sister-in-law'—the bitterness of her tone was like lemon on cold steel, and speaking, not to me, but to herself, she muttered, 'Nonsense, she would say—that's what they all say,' and while she spoke she fidgeted as though the skin on her back were as a plucked fowl's in a poulterer's shop-window.

'Oh that cow!' she broke off nervously, as though the great wooden cow in the meadow had shocked her and saved her from some indiscretion. Then she shuddered, and then she made the awkward angular movement that I had seen before, as if, after the spasm, some spot between the shoulders burnt or itched. Then again she looked the most unhappy woman in the world, and I once more reproached her, though not with the same conviction, for if there were a reason, and if I knew the reason, the stigma was removed from life.

'Sisters-in-law,' I said—

Her lips pursed as if to spit venom at the world; pursed they remained. All she did was to take her glove and rub hard at a spot on the window-pane. She rubbed as if she would rub something out for ever—some stain, some indelible contamination. Indeed, the spot remained for all her rubbing, and back she sank with the shudder and the clutch of the arm I had come to expect. Something impelled me to take my glove and rub my window. There, too, was a little speck on the glass. For all my rubbing it remained. And then the spasm went through me; I crooked my arm and plucked at the middle of my back.

My skin, too, felt like the damp chicken's skin in the poulterer's shop-window; one spot between the shoulders itched and irritated, felt clammy, felt raw. Could I reach it? Surreptitiously I tried. She saw me. A smile of infinite irony, infinite sorrow, flitted and faded from her face. But she had communicated, shared her secret, passed her poison; she would speak no more. Leaning back in my corner, shielding my eyes from her eyes, seeing only the slopes and hollows, greys and purples, of the winter's landscape, I read her message, deciphered her secret, reading it beneath her gaze.

Hilda's* the sister-in-law. Hilda? Hilda? Hilda Marsh—Hilda the blooming, the full bosomed, the matronly. Hilda stands at the door as the cab draws up, holding a coin. 'Poor Minnie,* more of a grasshopper than ever—old cloak she had last year. Well, well, with two children these days one can't do more. No, Minnie, I've got it; here you are, cabby—none of your ways with me. Come in, Minnie. Oh, I could carry *you*, let alone your basket!' So they go into the dining-room. 'Aunt Minnie, children.'

Slowly the knives and forks sink from the upright. Down they get (Bob and Barbara), hold out hands stiffly; back again to their chairs, staring between the resumed mouthfuls. [But this we'll skip; ornaments, curtains, trefoil china plate, yellow oblongs of cheese, white squares of biscuit—skip—oh, but wait! Half-way through luncheon one of those shivers; Bob stares at her, spoon in mouth. 'Get on with your pudding, Bob;' but Hilda disapproves. 'Why *should* she twitch?' Skip, skip, till we reach the landing on the upper floor; stairs brass-bound; linoleum worn; oh, yes! little bedroom looking out over the roofs of Eastbourne—zigzagging roofs like the spines of caterpillars, this way, that way, striped red and yellow, with blue-black slating.]

Now, Minnie, the door's shut; Hilda heavily descends to the basement; you unstrap the straps of your basket, lay on the bed a meagre nightgown, stand side by side furred felt slippers. The looking-glass—no, you avoid the looking-glass. Some methodical disposition of hat-pins. Perhaps the shell box has something in it? You shake it; it's the pearl stud there was last year—that's all. And then the sniff, the sigh, the sitting by the window. Three o'clock on a December after-noon; the rain drizzling; one light low in the skylight of a drapery emporium; another high in a servant's bedroom—this one goes out. That gives her nothing to look at. A moment's blankness—then, what are you thinking? (Let me peep across at her opposite; she's asleep or pretending it; so what would she think about sitting at the window at three o'clock in the afternoon? Health, money, hills, her God?) Yes, sitting on the very edge of the chair looking over the roofs of Eastbourne, Minnie Marsh prays to God. That's all very well; and she may rub the pane too, as though to see God better; but what God does she see? Who's the God of Minnie Marsh, the God of the back streets of Eastbourne, the God of the three o'clock in the afternoon? I, too, see roofs, I see sky; but, oh, dear—this seeing of Gods! More like President Kruger than Prince Albert*—that's the best I can do for him; and I see him on a chair, in a black frock-coat, not so very high up either; I can manage a cloud or two for him to sit on; and then his hand trailing in the cloud holds a rod, a truncheon is it?—black, thick, thorned—a brutal old bully—Minnie's God! Did he send the itch and the patch and the twitch? Is that why she prays? What she rubs on the window is the stain of sin. Oh, she committed some crime!

I have my choice of crimes. The woods flit and fly—in summer there are bluebells; in the opening there, when Spring comes, primroses. A parting, was it, twenty years ago? Vows broken? Not Minnie's! . . . She was faithful. How she nursed her mother! All her savings on the tombstone—wreaths under glass—daffodils in jars. But I'm off the track. A crime . . . They would say she kept her sorrow, suppressed her secret—her sex, they'd say—the scientific people. But what flummery to saddle *her* with sex! No—more like this. Passing down the streets of Croydon* twenty years ago, the violet loops of ribbon in the draper's window spangled in the electric light catch her eye. She lingers—past six. Still by running she can reach home. She pushes through the glass swing door. It's sale-time. Shallow trays brim with ribbons. She pauses, pulls this, fingers that with the raised roses on it—no need to choose, no need to buy, and each tray with its surprises. 'We don't shut till seven,' and then it *is* seven. She runs, she rushes, home she reaches, but too late. Neighbours—the doctor—baby brother—the kettle—scalded—hospital—dead—or only the shock of it, the blame? Ah, but the detail matters nothing! It's what she carries with her; the spot, the crime, the thing to expiate, always there between her shoulders. 'Yes,' she seems to nod to me, 'it's the thing I did.'

Whether you did, or what you did, I don't mind; it's not the thing I want. The draper's window looped with violet—that'll do; a little cheap perhaps, a little commonplace—since one has a choice of crimes, but then so many (let me peep across again—still sleeping, or pretending sleep! white, worn, the mouth closed—a touch of obstinacy, more than one would think—no hint of sex)—so many crimes aren't *your* crime; your crime was cheap; only the retribution solemn; for now the church door opens, the hard wooden pew receives her; on the brown tiles she kneels; every day, winter, summer, dusk, dawn (here she's at it) prays. All her sins fall, fall, for ever fall. The spot receives them. It's raised, it's red, it's burning. Next she twitches. Small boys point. 'Bob at lunch to-day'—But elderly women are the worst.

Indeed now you can't sit praying any longer. Kruger's sunk beneath the clouds—washed over as with a painter's brush of liquid grey, to which he adds a tinge of black—even the tip of the truncheon gone now. That's what always happens! Just as you've seen him, felt him, someone interrupts. It's Hilda now.

How you hate her! She'll even lock the bathroom door overnight, too, though it's only cold water you want, and sometimes when the night's been bad it seems as if washing helped. And John at breakfast—the children—meals are worst, and sometimes there are friends—ferns don't altogether hide 'em—they guess too; so out you go along the front, where the waves are grey, and the papers blow, and the glass shelters green and draughty, and the chairs cost tuppence—too much—for there must be preachers along the sands. Ah, that's a nigger—that's a funny man—that's a man with parakeets—poor little creatures! Is there no one here who thinks of God?—just up there, over the pier, with his rod—but no—there's nothing but grey in the sky or if it's blue the white clouds hide him, and the music—it's military music—and what are they fishing for? Do they catch them? How the children stare! Well, then home a back way—'Home a back way!' The words have meaning; might have been spoken by the old man with whiskers—no, no, he didn't really speak; but everything has meaning—placards leaning against doorways—names above shop-windows—red fruit in baskets—women's heads in the hairdresser's—all say 'Minnie Marsh!' But here's a jerk. 'Eggs are cheaper!' That's what always happens! I was heading her over the waterfall, straight for madness, when, like a flock of dream sheep, she turns t'other way and runs between my fingers. Eggs are cheaper. Tethered to the shores of the world, none of the crimes, sorrows, rhapsodies, or insanities for poor Minnie Marsh; never late for luncheon; never caught in a storm without a mackintosh; never utterly unconscious of the cheapness of eggs. So she reaches home—scrapes her boots.

Have I read you right? But the human face—the human face at the top of the fullest sheet of print holds more, withholds more. Now, eyes open, she looks out; and in the human eye—how d'you define it?—there's a break—a division—so that when you've grasped the stem the butterfly's off—the moth that hangs in the evening over the yellow flower—move, raise your hand, off, high, away. I won't raise my hand. Hang still, then, quiver, life, soul, spirit, whatever you are of Minnie Marsh—I, too, on my flower—the hawk over the down—alone, or what were the worth of life? To rise; hang still in the evening, in the midday; hang still over the down. The flicker of a hand—off, up! then poised again. Alone, unseen; seeing all so still down there, all so lovely. None seeing, none caring. The eyes of others our prisons; their thoughts our cages. Air above, air below. And the moon and immortality . . . Oh, but I drop to the turf! Are you down too, you in the corner, what's your name—woman—Minnie Marsh; some such name as that? There she is, tight to her blossom; opening her hand-bag, from which she takes a hollow shell—an egg—who was saying that eggs were cheaper? You or I? Oh, it was you who said it on the way home, you remember, when the old gentleman, suddenly opening his umbrella—or sneezing was it? Anyhow, Kruger went, and you came 'home a back way,' and scraped your boots. Yes. And now you lay across your knees a pocket-handkerchief into which drop little angular fragments of eggshell—fragments of a map—a puzzle. I wish I could piece them together! If you would only sit still. She's moved her knees—the map's in bits again. Down the slopes of the Andes the white blocks of marble go bounding and hurtling, crushing to death a whole troop of Spanish muleteers, with their convoy—Drake's booty, gold and silver,* But to return—

To what, to where? She opened the door, and, putting her umbrella in the stand—that goes without saying; so, too, the whiff of beef from the basement; dot, dot, dot. But what I cannot thus eliminate, what I must, head down, eyes shut, with the courage of a battalion and the blindness of a bull, charge and disperse are, indubitably, the figures behind the ferns, commercial travellers. There I've hidden them all this time in the hope that somehow they'd disappear, or better still emerge, as indeed they must, if the story's to go on gathering richness and rotundity, destiny and tragedy, as stories should, rolling along with it two, if not three, commercial travellers and a whole grove of aspidistra. 'The fronds of the aspidistra only partly concealed the commercial traveller—' Rhododendrons would conceal him utterly, and into the bargain give me my fling of red and white, for which I starve and strive; but rhododendrons in Eastbourne—in December—on the Marshes' table—no, no, I dare not; it's all a matter of crusts and cruets, frills and ferns. Perhaps there'll be a moment later by the sea. Moreover, I feel, pleasantly pricking through the green fretwork and over the glacis* of cut glass, a desire to peer and peep at the man opposite—one's as much as I can manage. James Moggridge is it, whom the Marshes call Jimmy? [Minnie you must promise not to twitch till I've got this straight.] James Moggridge travels in—shall we say buttons?*—but the time's not come for bringing *them* in—the big and the little on the long cards, some peacock-eyed, others dull gold; cairngorms some, and others coral sprays—but I say the time's not come. He travels, and on Thursdays, his Eastbourne day, takes his meals with the Marshes. His red face, his little steady eyes—by no means altogether commonplace—his enormous appetite (that's safe; he won't look at Minnie till the bread's swamped the gravy dry), napkin tucked diamond-wise—but this is primitive, and, whatever it may do the reader, don't take me in. Let's dodge to the Moggridge household, set that in motion. Well, the family boots are mended on Sundays by James himself. He reads *Truth*.* But his passion? Roses—and his wife a retired hospital nurse—interesting—for God's sake let me have one woman with a name I like! But no; she's of the unborn children of the mind, illicit, none the less loved, like my rhododendrons. How many die in every novel that's written—the best, the dearest, while Moggridge lives. It's life's fault. Here's Minnie eating her egg at the moment opposite and at t'other end of the line—are we past Lewes?—there must be Jimmy—or what's her twitch for?

There must be Moggridge—life's fault. Life imposes her laws; life blocks the way; life's behind the fern; life's the tyrant; oh, but not the bully! No, for I assure you I come willingly; I come wooed by Heaven knows what compulsion across ferns and cruets, table splashed and bottles smeared. I come irresistibly to lodge myself somewhere on the firm flesh, in the robust spine, wherever I can penetrate or find foothold on the person, in the soul, of Moggridge the man. The enormous stability of the fabric; the spine tough as whalebone, straight as oak-tree; the ribs radiating branches; the flesh taut tarpaulin; the red hollows; the suck and regurgitation of the heart; while from above meat falls in brown cubes and beer gushes to be churned to blood again—and so we reach the eyes. Behind the aspidistra they see something: black, white, dismal; now the plate again; behind the aspidistra they see elderly woman; 'Marsh's sister, Hilda's more my sort;' the tablecloth now. 'Marsh would know what's wrong with Morrises . . .' talk that over; cheese has come; the plate again; turn it round—the enormous fingers; now the woman opposite. 'Marsh's sister—not a bit like Marsh; wretched elderly female . . . You should feed your hens . . . God's truth, what's set her twitching? Not what *I* said? Dear, dear, dear! these elderly women. Dear, dear!'

[Yes, Minnie; I know you've twitched, but one moment—James Moggridge.]

'Dear, dear, dear!' How beautiful the sound is! like the knock of a mallet on seasoned timber, like the throb of the heart of an ancient whaler when the seas press thick and the green is clouded. 'Dear, dear!' what a passing bell for the souls of the fretful to soothe them and solace them, lap them in linen, saying, 'So long. Good luck to you!' and then, 'What's your pleasure?' for though Moggridge would pluck his rose for her, that's done, that's over. Now what's the next thing? 'Madam, you'll miss your train,' for they don't linger.

That's the man's way; that's the sound that reverberates; that's St Paul's* and the motor-omnibuses. But we're brushing the crumbs off. Oh, Moggridge, you won't stay? You must be off? Are you driving through Eastbourne this afternoon in one of those little carriages? Are you the man who's walled up in green cardboard boxes, and sometimes has the blinds down, and sometimes sits so solemn staring like a sphinx, and always there's a look of the sepulchral, something of the undertaker, the coffin, and the dusk about horse and driver? Do tell me—but the doors slammed. We shall never meet again. Moggridge, farewell!

Yes, yes, I'm coming. Right up to the top of the house. One moment I'll linger. How the mud goes round in the mind—what a swirl these monsters leave, the waters rocking, the weeds waving and green here, black there, striking to the sand, till by degrees the atoms reassemble, the deposit sifts itself, and again through the eyes one sees clear and still, and there comes to the lips some prayer for the departed, some obsequy for the souls of those one nods to, the people one never meets again.

James Moggridge is dead now, gone for ever. Well, Minnie—'I can face it no longer.' If she said that—(Let me look at her. She is brushing the eggshell into deep declivities). She said it certainly, leaning against the wall of the bedroom, and plucking at the little balls which edge the claret-coloured curtain. But when the self speaks to the self, who is speaking?—the entombed soul, the spirit driven in, in, in to the central catacomb; the self that took the veil and left the world—a coward perhaps, yet somehow beautiful, as it flits with its lantern restlessly up and down the dark corridors. 'I can bear it no longer,' her spirit says. 'That man at lunch—Hilda—the children.' Oh, heavens, her sob! It's the spirit wailing its destiny, the spirit driven hither, thither, lodging on the diminishing carpets—meagre footholds—shrunken shreds of all the vanishing universe—love, life, faith, husband, children, I know not what splendours and pageantries glimpsed in girlhood. 'Not for me—not for me.'

But then—the muffins, the bald elderly dog? Bead mats I should fancy and the consolation of underlinen. If Minnie Marsh were run over and taken to hospital, nurses and doctors themselves would exclaim ... There's the vista and the vision—there's the distance—the blue blot at the end of the avenue, while, after all, the tea is rich, the muffin hot, and the dog—'Benny, to your basket, sir, and see what mother's brought you!' So, taking the glove with the worn thumb, defying once more the encroaching demon of what's called going in holes, you renew the fortifications, threading the grey wool, running it in and out.

Running it in and out, across and over, spinning a web through which God himself—hush, don't think of God! How firm the stitches are! You must be proud of your darning. Let nothing disturb her. Let the light fall gently, and the clouds show an inner vest of the first green leaf. Let the sparrow perch on the twig and shake the raindrop hanging to the twig's elbow . . . Why look up? Was it a sound, a thought? Oh, heavens! Back again to the thing you did, the plate glass with the violet loops? But Hilda will come. Ignominies, humiliations, oh! Close the breach.

Having mended her glove, Minnie Marsh lays it in the drawer. She shuts the drawer with decision. I catch sight of her face in the glass. Lips are pursed. Chin held high. Next she laces her shoes. Then she touches her throat. What's your brooch? Mistletoe or merrythought?* And what is happening? Unless I'm much mistaken, the pulse's quickened, the moments coming, the threads are racing, Niagara's ahead. Here's the crisis! Heaven be with you! Down she goes. Courage, courage! Face it, be it! For God's sake don't wait on the mat now! There's the door! I'm on your side. Speak! Confront her, confound her soul!

'Oh, I beg your pardon! Yes, this is Eastbourne. I'll reach it down for you. Let me try the handle.' [But, Minnie, though we keep up pretences, I've read you right—I'm with you now.]

'That's all your luggage?'

'Much obliged, I'm sure.'

(But why do you look about you? Hilda won't come to the station, nor John; and Moggridge is driving at the far side of Eastbourne.)

'I'll wait by my bag, ma'am, that's safest. He said he'd meet me . . . Oh, there he is! That's my son.'

So they walk off together.

Well, but I'm confounded . . . Surely Minnie, you know better! A strange young man . . . Stop! I'll tell him—Minnie!—Miss Marsh!—I don't know though. There's something queer in her cloak as it blows. Oh, but it's untrue, it's indecent . . . Look how he bends as they reach the gateway. She finds her ticket. What's the joke? Off they go, down the road, side by side . . . Well, my world's done for! What do I stand on? What do I know? That's not Minnie. There never was Moggridge. Who am I? Life's bare as bone.

And yet the last look of them—he stepping from the kerb and she following him round the edge of the big building brims me with won-der—floods me anew. Mysterious figures! Mother and son. Who are you? Why do you walk down the street? Where to-night will you sleep, and then, to-morrow? Oh, how it whirls and surges—floats me afresh! I start after them. People drive this way and that. The white light splutters and pours. Plate-glass windows. Carnations; chrysanthe-mums. Ivy in dark gardens. Milk carts at the door. Wherever I go, mysterious figures, I see you, turning the corner, mothers and sons; you, you, you. I hasten, I follow. This, I fancy, must be the sea. Grey is the landscape; dim as ashes; the water murmurs and moves. If I fall on my knees, if I go through the ritual, the ancient antics, it's you, unknown figures, you I adore; if I open my arms, it's you I embrace, you I draw to me—adorable world!

SOLID OBJECTS

THE only thing that moved upon the vast semi-circle of the beach was one small black spot. As it came nearer to the ribs and spine of the stranded pilchard boat,* it became apparent from a certain tenuity in its blackness that this spot possessed four legs; and moment by moment it became more unmistakable that it was composed of the persons of two young men. Even thus in outline against the sand there was an unmistakable vitality in them; an indescribable vigour in the approach and withdrawal of the bodies, slight though it was, which proclaimed some violent argument issuing from the tiny mouths of the little round heads. This was corroborated on closer view by the repeated lunging of a walking-stick on the right-hand side. 'You mean to tell me . . . You actually believe . . .' thus the walking-stick on the right-hand side next the waves seemed to be asserting as it cut long straight stripes upon the sand.

'Politics be damned!'* issued clearly from the body on the left-hand side, and, as these words were uttered, the mouths, noses, chins, little moustaches, tweed caps, rough boots, shooting coats, and check stockings of the two speakers became clearer and clearer; the smoke of their pipes went up into the air; nothing was so solid, so living, so hard, red, hirsute and virile as these two bodies for miles and miles of sea and sandhill.

They flung themselves down by the six ribs and spine of the black pilchard boat. You know how the body seems to shake itself free from an argument, and to apologize for a mood of exaltation; flinging itself down and expressing in the looseness of its attitude a readiness to take up with something new—whatever it may be that comes next to hand. So Charles, whose stick had been slashing the beach for half a mile or so, began skimming flat pieces of slate over the water; and John, who had exclaimed 'Politics be damned!' began burrowing his fingers down, down, into the sand. As his hand went further and further beyond the wrist, so that he had to hitch his sleeve a little higher, his eyes lost their intensity, or rather the background of thought and experience which gives an inscrutable depth to the eyes of grown people disappeared, leaving only the clear transparent surface, expressing nothing but wonder, which the eyes of young children display. No doubt the act of burrowing in the sand had something to do with it. He remembered that, after digging for a little, the water oozes round your finger-tips; the hole then becomes a moat; a well; a spring; a secret channel to the sea. As he was choosing which of these things to make it, still working his fingers in the water, they curled round something hard—a full drop of solid matter—and gradually dislodged a large irregular lump, and brought it to the surface. When the sand coating was wiped off, a green tint appeared. It was a lump of glass, so thick as to be almost opaque; the smoothing of the sea had completely worn off any edge or shape, so that it was impossible to say whether it had been bottle, tumbler or window-pane; it was nothing but glass; it was almost a precious stone. You had only to enclose it in a rim of gold, or pierce it with a wire, and it became a jewel; part of a necklace, or a dull, green light upon a finger. Perhaps after all it was really a gem; something worn by a dark Princess trailing her finger in the water as she sat in the stern of the boat and listened to the slaves singing as they rowed her across the Bay. Or the oak sides of a sunk Elizabethan treasure-chest had split apart, and, rolled over and over, over and over, its emeralds had come at last to shore. John turned it in his hands; he held it to the light; he held it so that its irregular mass blotted out the body and extended right arm of his friend. The green thinned and thickened slightly as it was held against the sky or against the body. It pleased him; it puzzled him; it was so hard, so concentrated, so definite an object compared with the vague sea and the hazy shore.

Now a sigh disturbed him—profound, final, making him aware that his friend Charles had thrown all the flat stones within reach, or had come to the conclusion that it was not worth while to throw them. They ate their sandwiches side by side. When they had done, and were shaking themselves and rising to their feet, John took the lump of glass and looked at it in silence. Charles looked at it too. But he saw immediately that it was not flat, and filling his pipe he said with the energy that dismisses a foolish strain of thought,

'To return to what I was saying—'

He did not see, or if he had seen would hardly have noticed, that John after looking at the lump for a moment, as if in hesitation, slipped it inside his pocket. That impulse, too, may have been the impulse which leads a child to pick up one pebble on a path strewn with them, promising it a life of warmth and security upon the

nursery mantelpiece, delighting in the sense of power and benignity
which such an action confers, and believing that the heart of the stone
leaps with joy when it sees itself chosen from a million like it, to enjoy
this bliss instead of a life of cold and wet upon the high road. 'It might
so easily have been any other of the millions of stones, but it was I, I, I!'

Whether this thought or not was in John's mind: the lump of glass
had its place upon the mantelpiece, where it stood heavy upon a little
pile of bills and letters, and served not only as an excellent paper-
weight, but also as a natural stopping place for the young man's eyes
when they wandered from his book. Looked at again and again half
consciously by a mind thinking of something else, any object mixes
itself so profoundly with the stuff of thought that it loses its actual
form and recomposes itself a little differently in an ideal shape which
haunts the brain when we least expect it. So John found himself
attracted to the windows of curiosity shops when he was out walking,
merely because he saw something which reminded him of the lump of
glass. Anything, so long as it was an object of some kind, more or less
round, perhaps with a dying flame deep sunk in its mass, anything—china, glass, amber, rock, marble—even the smooth oval egg
of a prehistoric bird would do. He took, also, to keeping his eyes upon
the ground, especially in the neighbourhood of waste land where the
household refuse is thrown away. Such objects often occurred
there—thrown away, of no use to anybody, shapeless, discarded. In
a few months he had collected four or five specimens that took their
place upon the mantelpiece. They were useful, too, for a man who is
standing for Parliament upon the brink of a brilliant career has any
number of papers to keep in order—addresses to constituents, dec-
larations of policy, appeals for subscriptions, invitations to dinner,
and so on.

One day, starting from his rooms in the Temple* to catch a train in
order to address his constituents, his eyes rested upon a remarkable
object lying half-hidden in one of those little borders of grass which
edge the bases of vast legal buildings. He could only touch it with the
point of his stick through the railings; but he could see that it was
a piece of china of the most remarkable shape, as nearly resembling
a starfish as anything—shaped, or broken accidentally, into five
irregular but unmistakable points. The colouring was mainly blue,
but green stripes or spots of some kind overlaid the blue, and lines of
crimson gave it a richness and lustre of the most attractive kind. John

was determined to possess it; but the more he pushed, the further it receded. At length he was forced to go back to his rooms and improvise a wire ring attached to the end of a stick, with which, by dint of great care and skill, he finally drew the piece of china within reach of his hands. As he seized hold of it he exclaimed in triumph. At that moment the clock struck. It was out of the question that he should keep his appointment. The meeting was held without him. But how had the piece of china been broken into this remarkable shape? A careful examination put it beyond doubt that the star shape was accidental, which made it all the more strange, and it seemed unlikely that there should be another such in existence. Set at the opposite end of the mantelpiece from the lump of glass that had been dug from the sand, it looked like a creature from another world—freakish and fantastic as a harlequin. It seemed to be pirouetting through space; winking light like a fitful star. The contrast between the china so vivid and alert, and the glass so mute and contemplative, fascinated him, and wondering and amazed he asked himself how the two came to exist in the same world, let alone to stand upon the same narrow strip of marble in the same room. The question remained unanswered.

He now began to haunt the places which are most prolific of broken china, such as pieces of waste land between railway lines, sites of demolished houses, and commons in the neighbourhood of London. But china is seldom thrown from a great height; it is one of the rarest of human actions. You have to find in conjunction a very high house, and a woman of such reckless impulse and passionate prejudice that she flings her jar or pot straight from the window without thought of who is below. Broken china was to be found in plenty, but broken in some trifling domestic accident, without purpose or character. Nevertheless, he was often astonished, as he came to go into the question more deeply, by the immense variety of shapes to be found in London alone, and there was still more cause for wonder and speculation in the differences of qualities and designs. The finest specimens he would bring home and place upon his mantelpiece, where, however, their duty was more and more of an ornamental nature, since papers needing a weight to keep them down became scarcer and scarcer.

He neglected his duties, perhaps, or discharged them absent-mindedly, or his constituents when they visited him were unfavourably impressed by the appearance of his mantelpiece. At any rate he was not elected to represent them in Parliament, and his friend

Charles, taking it much to heart and hurrying to condole with him, found him so little cast down by the disaster that he could only suppose that it was too serious a matter for him to realize all at once.

In truth, John had been that day to Barnes Common,* and there under a furse bush had found a very remarkable piece of iron. It was almost identical with the glass in shape, massy and globular, but so cold and heavy, so black and metallic, that it was evidently alien to the earth and had its origin in one of the dead stars or was itself the cinder of a moon. It weighed his pocket down; it weighed the mantelpiece down; it radiated cold. And yet the meteorite stood upon the same ledge with the lump of glass and the star-shaped china.

As his eyes passed from one to another, the determination to possess objects that even surpassed these tormented the young man. He devoted himself more and more resolutely to the search. If he had not been consumed by ambition and convinced that one day some newly-discovered rubbish heap would reward him, the disappointments he had suffered, let alone the fatigue and derision, would have made him give up the pursuit. Provided with a bag and a long stick fitted with an adaptable hook, he ransacked all deposits of earth; raked beneath matted tangles of scrub; searched all alleys and spaces between walls where he had learned to expect to find objects of this kind thrown away. As his standard became higher and his taste more severe the disappointments were innumerable, but always some gleam of hope, some piece of china or glass curiously marked or broken, lured him on. Day after day passed. He was no longer young. His career—that is, his political career—was a thing of the past. People gave up visiting him. He was too silent to be worth asking to dinner. He never talked to anyone about his serious ambitions; their lack of understanding was apparent in their behaviour.

He leaned back in his chair now and watched Charles lift the stones on the mantelpiece a dozen times and put them down emphatically to mark what he was saying about the conduct of the Government, without once noticing their existence.

'What was the truth of it, John?' asked Charles suddenly, turning and facing him. 'What made you give it up like that all in a second?'

'I've not given it up,' John replied.

'But you've not the ghost of a chance now,' said Charles roughly.

'I don't agree with you there,' said John with conviction. Charles looked at him and was profoundly uneasy; the most extraordinary doubts possessed him; he had a queer sense that they were talking about different things. He looked round to find some relief for his horrible depression, but the disorderly appearance of the room depressed him still further. What was that stick, and the old carpet bag hanging against the wall? And then those stones? Looking at John, something fixed and distant in his expression alarmed him. He knew only too well that his mere appearance upon a platform was out of the question.

'Pretty stones,' he said as cheerfully as he could; and saying that he had an appointment to keep, he left John—for ever.

A HAUNTED HOUSE

WHATEVER hour you woke there was a door shutting. From room to room they went, hand in hand, lifting here, opening there, making sure—a ghostly couple.

'Here we left it,' she said. And he added, 'Oh, but here too!' 'It's upstairs,' she murmured. 'And in the garden,' he whispered. 'Quietly,' they said, 'or we shall wake them.'

But it wasn't that you woke us. Oh, no. 'They're looking for it; they're drawing the curtain' one might say, and so read on a page or two. 'Now they've found it,' one would be certain, stopping the pencil on the margin. And then, tired of reading, one might rise and see for oneself, the house all empty, the doors standing open, only the wood pigeons bubbling with content and the hum of the threshing machine sounding from the farm. 'What did I come in here for? What did I want to find?' My hands were empty. 'Perhaps it's upstairs then?' The apples were in the loft. And so down again, the garden still as ever, only the book had slipped into the grass.

But they had found it in the drawing-room. Not that one could ever see them. The window panes reflected apples, reflected roses; all the leaves were green in the glass. If they moved in the drawing-room, the apple only turned its yellow side. Yet, the moment after, if the door was opened, spread about the floor, hung upon the walls, pendant from the ceiling—what? My hands were empty. The shadow of a thrush crossed the carpet; from the deepest wells of silence the wood pigeon drew its bubble of sound. 'Safe, safe, safe,' the pulse of the house beat softly. 'The treasure buried; the room . . .' the pulse stopped short. Oh, was that the buried treasure?

A moment later the light had faded. Out in the garden then? But the trees spun darkness for a wandering beam of sun. So fine, so rare, coolly sunk beneath the surface the beam I sought always burnt behind the glass. Death was the glass; death was between us; coming to the woman first, hundreds of years ago, leaving the house, sealing all the windows; the rooms were darkened. He left it, left her, went North, went East, saw the stars turned in the Southern sky; sought the house, found it dropped beneath the Downs.* 'Safe, safe, safe,' the pulse of the house beat gladly, 'The treasure yours.'

The wind roars up the avenue. Trees stoop and bend this way and that. Moonbeams splash and spill wildly in the rain. But the beam of the lamp falls straight from the window. The candle burns stiff and still. Wandering through the house, opening the windows, whispering not to wake us, the ghostly couple seek their joy.

'Here we slept,' she says. And he adds, 'Kisses without number.' 'Waking in the morning—' 'Silver between the trees—' 'Upstairs—' 'In the garden—' 'When summer came—' 'In winter snowtime—' The doors go shutting far in the distance, gently knocking like the pulse of a heart.

Nearer they come; cease at the doorway. The wind falls, the rain slides silver down the glass. Our eyes darken; we hear no steps beside us; we see no lady spread her ghostly cloak. His hands shield the lantern. 'Look,' he breathes. 'Sound asleep. Love upon their lips.'

Stooping, holding their silver lamp above us, long they look and deeply. Long they pause. The wind drives straightly; the flame stoops slightly. Wild beams of moonlight cross both floor and wall, and, meeting, stain the faces bent; the faces pondering; the faces that search the sleepers and seek their hidden joy.

'Safe, safe, safe,' the heart of the house beats proudly. 'Long years—' he sighs. 'Again you found me.' 'Here,' she murmurs, 'sleeping; in the garden reading; laughing, rolling apples in the loft. Here we left our treasure—' Stooping, their light lifts the lids upon my eyes. 'Safe! safe! safe!' the pulse of the house beats wildly. Waking, I cry 'Oh, is *this* your buried treasure? The light in the heart.'

MONDAY OR TUESDAY

LAZY and indifferent, shaking space easily from his wings, knowing his way, the heron passes over the church beneath the sky. White and distant, absorbed in itself, endlessly the sky covers and uncovers, moves and remains. A lake? Blot the shores of it out! A mountain? Oh, perfect—the sun gold on its slopes. Down that falls. Ferns then, or white feathers, for ever and ever—

Desiring truth, awaiting it, laboriously distilling a few words, for ever desiring—(a cry starts to the left, another to the right. Wheels strike divergently. Omnibuses conglomerate in conflict)—for ever desiring—(the clock asseverates with twelve distinct strokes that it is midday,* light sheds gold scales; children swarm)—for ever desiring truth. Red is the dome; coins hang on the trees; smoke trails from the chimneys; bark, shout, cry 'Iron for sale'—and truth?

Radiating to a point men's feet and women's feet, black or gold-encrusted—(This foggy weather—Sugar? No, thank you—The commonwealth of the future)—the firelight darting and making the room red, save for the black figures and their bright eyes, while outside a van discharges, Miss Thingummy drinks tea at her desk, and plate-glass preserves fur coats—

Flaunted, leaf-light, drifting at corners, blown across the wheels, silver-splashed, home or not home, gathered, scattered, squandered in separate scales, swept up, down, torn, sunk, assembled*—and truth?

Now to recollect by the fireside on the white square of marble. From ivory depths words rising shed their blackness, blossom and penetrate. Fallen the book; in the flame, in the smoke, in the momentary sparks—or now voyaging, the marble square pendant, minarets beneath and the India seas, while space rushes blue and stars glint—truth? or now, content with closeness?

Lazy and indifferent the heron returns; the sky veils her stars; then bares them.

BLUE & GREEN

Green

THE pointed fingers of glass hang downwards. The light slides down the glass, and drops a pool of green. All day long the ten fingers of the lustre* drop green upon the marble. The feathers of parakeets—their harsh cries—sharp blades of palm trees—green too; green needles glittering in the sun. But the hard glass drips on to the marble; the pools hover above the desert sand; the camels lurch through them; the pools settle on the marble; rushes edge them; weeds clog them; here and there a white blossom; the frog flops over; at night the stars are set there unbroken. Evening comes, and the shadow sweeps the green over the mantelpiece; the ruffled surface of ocean. No ships come; the aimless waves sway beneath the empty sky. It's night; the needles drip blots of blue. The green's out.

BLUE & GREEN

Blue

THE snub-nosed monster rises to the surface and spouts through his blunt nostrils two columns of water, which, fiery-white in the centre, spray off into a fringe of blue beads. Strokes of blue line the black tarpaulin of his hide. Slushing the water through mouth and nostrils he sinks, heavy with water, and the blue closes over him dowsing the polished pebbles of his eyes. Thrown upon the beach he lies, blunt, obtuse, shedding dry blue scales. Their metallic blue stains the rusty iron on the beach. Blue are the ribs of the wrecked rowing boat. A wave rolls beneath the blue bells. But the cathedral's different, cold, incense laden, faint blue with the veils of madonnas.

THE STRING QUARTET

WELL, here we are, and if you cast your eye over the room you will see that Tubes and trams and omnibuses, private carriages not a few, even, I venture to believe, landaus with bays* in them, have been busy at it, weaving threads from one end of London to the other. Yet I begin to have my doubts—

If indeed it's true, as they're saying, that Regent Street is up, and the Treaty signed,* and the weather not cold for the time of year, and even at that rent not a flat to be had, and the worst of influenza* is after effects; if I bethink me of having forgotten to write about the leak in the larder, and left my glove in the train; if the ties of blood require me, leaning forward, to accept cordially the hand which is perhaps offered hesitatingly—

'Seven years since we met!'

'The last time in Venice.'

'And where are you living now?'

'Well, the late afternoon suits me the best, though, if it weren't asking too much—'

'But I knew you at once!'

'Still, the war made a break—'

If the mind's shot through by such little arrows, and—for human society compels it—no sooner is one launched than another presses forward; if this engenders heat and in addition they've turned on the electric light; if saying one thing does, in so many cases, leave behind it a need to improve and revise, stirring besides regrets, pleasures, vanities, and desires—if it's all the facts I mean, and the hats, the fur boas, the gentlemen's swallowtail coats, and pearl tie-pins that come to the surface—what chance is there?

Of what? It becomes every minute more difficult to say why, in spite of everything, I sit here believing I can't now say what, or even remember the last time it happened.

'Did you see the procession?'

'The King* looked cold.'

No, no, no. But what was it?

'She's bought a house at Malmesbury.'*

'How lucky to find one!'

On the contrary, it seems to me pretty sure that she, whoever she may be, is damned, since it's all a matter of flats and hats and sea gulls, or so it seems to be for a hundred people sitting here well dressed, walled in, furred, replete. Not that I can boast, since I too sit passive on a gilt chair, only turning the earth above a buried memory, as we all do, for there are signs, if I'm not mistaken, that we're all recalling something, furtively seeking something. Why fidget? Why so anxious about the sit of cloaks; and gloves—whether to button or unbutton? Then watch that elderly face against the dark canvas, a moment ago urbane and flushed; now taciturn and sad, as if in shadow. Was it the sound of the second violin tuning in the ante-room? Here they come; four black figures, carrying instruments, and seat themselves facing the white squares under the downpour of light; rest the tips of their bows on the music stand; with a simultaneous movement lift them; lightly poise them, and, looking across at the player opposite, the first violin counts one, two, three—

Flourish, spring, burgeon, burst! The pear tree on the top of the mountain. Fountains jet; drops descend. But the waters of the Rhone flow swift and deep, race under the arches, and sweep the trailing water leaves, washing shadows over the silver fish, the spotted fish rushed down by the swift waters, now swept into an eddy where—it's difficult this—conglomeration of fish all in a pool; leaping, splashing, scraping sharp fins; and such a boil of current that the yellow pebbles are churned round and round, round and round—free now, rushing downwards, or even somehow ascending in exquisite spirals into the air; curled like thin shavings from under a plane; up and up . . . How lovely goodness is in those who, stepping lightly, go smiling through the world! Also in old, jolly fishwives, squatted under arches, obscene old women,* how deeply they laugh and shake and rollick, when they walk, from side to side, hum, hah!

'That's an early Mozart, of course—'

'But the tune, like all his tunes, makes one despair—I mean hope. What do I mean? That's the worst of music! I want to dance, laugh, eat pink cakes, yellow cakes, drink thin, sharp wine. Or an indecent story, now—I could relish that. The older one grows the more one likes indecency. Hah, hah! I'm laughing. What at? You said nothing, nor did the old gentleman opposite . . . But suppose—suppose—Hush!'

The melancholy river bears us on. When the moon comes through the trailing willow boughs, I see your face, I hear your voice and the bird singing as we pass the osier bed. What are you whispering? Sorrow, sorrow. Joy, joy. Woven together* like reeds in moonlight. Woven together, inextricably commingled, bound in pain and strewn in sorrow—crash!

The boat sinks. Rising, the figures ascend, but now leaf thin, tapering to a dusky wraith, which, fiery tipped, draws its twofold passion from my heart. For me it sings, unseals my sorrow, thaws compassion, floods with love the sunless world, nor ceasing, abates its tenderness but deftly, subtly, weaves in and out until in this pattern, this consummation, the cleft ones unify; soar, sob, sink to rest, sorrow and joy:

Why then grieve? Ask what? Remain unsatisfied? I say all's been settled; yes; laid to rest under a coverlet of rose leaves, falling. Falling. Ah, but they cease. One rose leaf, falling from an enormous height, like a little parachute dropped from an invisible balloon, turns, flutters waveringly. It won't reach us.

'No, no. I noticed nothing. That's the worst of music—these silly dreams. The second violin was late, you say?'

'There's old Mrs Munro, feeling her way out—blinder each year, poor woman—on this slippery floor.'

Eyeless old age, grey-headed Sphinx . . . There she stands on the pavement, beckoning, so sternly to the red omnibus.

'How lovely! How well they play! How—how—how!'

The tongue is but a clapper. Simplicity itself. The feathers in the hat next to me are bright and pleasing as a child's rattle. The leaf on the plane-tree flashes green through the chink in the curtain. Very strange, very exciting.

'How—how—how!' Hush!

These are the lovers on the grass.

'If, madam, you will take my hand—'

'Sir, I would trust you with my heart. Moreover, we have left our bodies in the banqueting hall. Those on the turf are the shadows of our souls.'

'Then these are the embraces of our souls.' The lemons nod assent. The swan pushes from the bank and floats dreaming into mid stream.

'But to return. He followed me down the corridor, and, as we turned the corner, trod on the lace of my petticoat. What could I do but cry ("Ah!") and stop to finger it? At which he drew his sword, made passes as if he were stabbing something to death, and cried, "Mad! Mad! Mad!" Whereupon I screamed, and the Prince, who was writing in the large vellum book in the oriel window, came out in his velvet skull-cap and furred slippers, snatched a rapier from the wall—the King of Spain's gift, you know—on which I escaped, flinging on this cloak to hide the ravages to my skirt—to hide . . . But listen! the horns!'

The gentleman replies so fast to the lady, and she runs up the scale with such witty exchange of compliment now culminating in a sob of passion, that the words are indistinguishable though the meaning is plain enough—love, laughter, flight, pursuit, celestial bliss—all floated out on the gayest ripple of tender endearment—until the sound of the silver horns, at first far distant, gradually sounds more and more distinctly, as if seneschals* were saluting the dawn or proclaiming ominously the escape of the lovers . . . The green garden, moonlit pool, lemons, lovers, and fish are all dissolved in the opal sky, across which, as the horns are joined by trumpets and supported by clarions there rise white arches firmly planted on marble pillars . . . Tramp and trumpeting. Clang and clangour. Firm establishment. Fast foundations. March of myriads. Confusion and chaos trod to earth. But this city to which we travel has neither stone nor marble; hangs enduring; stands unshakable; nor does a face, nor does a flag greet or welcome. Leave then to perish your hope; droop in the desert my joy; naked advance. Bare are the pillars; auspicious to none; casting no shade; resplendent; severe. Back then I fall, eager no more, desiring only to go, find the street, mark the buildings, greet the applewoman, say to the maid who opens the door: A starry night.

'Good night, good night. You go this way?'

'Alas. I go that.'

A SOCIETY

THIS is how it all came about. Six or seven of us were sitting one day after tea. Some were gazing across the street into the windows of a milliner's shop where the light still shone brightly upon scarlet feathers and golden slippers. Others were idly occupied in building little towers of sugar upon the edge of the tea tray. After a time, so far as I can remember, we drew round the fire and began as usual to praise men—how strong, how noble, how brilliant, how courageous, how beautiful they were—how we envied those who by hook or by crook managed to get attached to one for life—when Poll, who had said nothing, burst into tears. Poll, I must tell you, has always been queer. For one thing her father was a strange man. He left her a fortune in his will, but on condition that she read all the books in the London Library.* We comforted her as best we could; but we knew in our hearts how vain it was. For though we like her, Poll is no beauty; leaves her shoe laces untied; and must have been thinking, while we praised men, that not one of them would ever wish to marry her. At last she dried her tears. For some time we could make nothing of what she said. Strange enough it was in all conscience. She told us that, as we knew, she spent most of her time in the London Library, reading. She had begun, she said, with English literature on the top floor; and was steadily working her way down to *The Times* on the bottom. And now half, or perhaps only a quarter, way through a terrible thing had happened. She could read no more. Books were not what we thought them. 'Books' she cried, rising to her feet and speaking with an intensity of desolation which I shall never forget, 'are for the most part unutterably bad!'

Of course we cried out that Shakespeare wrote books, and Milton and Shelley.

'Oh yes,' she interrupted us. 'You've been well taught, I can see. But you are not members of the London Library.' Here her sobs broke forth anew. At length, recovering a little, she opened one of the pile of books which she always carried about with her—'From a Window' or 'In a Garden' or some such name as that it was called, and it was written by a man called Benton or Henson or something of that kind.* She read the first few pages. We listened in silence. 'But that's not a book,' someone said. So she chose another. This time it was a history, but I have forgotten the writer's name. Our trepidation increased as she went on. Not a word of it seemed to be true, and the style in which it was written was execrable.

'Poetry! Poetry!' we cried, impatiently. 'Read us poetry!' I cannot describe the desolation which fell upon us as she opened a little volume and mouthed out the verbose, sentimental foolery which it contained.

'It must have been written by a woman' one of us urged. But no. She told us that it was written by a young man, one of the most famous poets of the day. I leave you to imagine what the shock of the discovery was. Though we all cried and begged her to read no more she persisted and read us extracts from the Lives of the Lord Chancellors.* When she had finished, Jane, the eldest and wisest of us, rose to her feet and said that she for one was not convinced.

'Why' she asked 'if men write such rubbish as this, should our mothers have wasted their youth in bringing them into the world?'

We were all silent; and in the silence, poor Poll could be heard sobbing out, 'Why, why did my father teach me to read?'

Clorinda* was the first to come to her senses. 'It's all our fault' she said. 'Every one of us knows how to read. But no one, save Poll, has ever taken the trouble to do it. I, for one, have taken it for granted that it was a woman's duty to spend her youth in bearing children. I venerated my mother for bearing ten; still more my grandmother for bearing fifteen; it was, I confess, my own ambition to bear twenty. We have gone on all these ages supposing that men were equally industrious, and that their works were of equal merit. While we have borne the children, they, we supposed, have borne the books and the pictures. We have populated the world. They have civilized it. But now that we can read, what prevents us from judging the results? Before we bring another child into the world we must swear that we will find out what the world is like.'

So we made ourselves into a society for asking questions. One of us was to visit a man-of-war; another was to hide herself in a scholar's study; another was to attend a meeting of business men; while all were to read books, look at pictures, go to concerts, keep our eyes open in the streets; and ask questions perpetually. We were very young. You can judge of our simplicity when I tell you that before parting that night we agreed that the objects of life were to produce good people and good books.* Our questions were to be directed to finding out how far these objects were now attained by men. We vowed solemnly that we would not bear a single child until we were satisfied.

Off we went then, some to the British Museum; others to the King's Navy; some to Oxford; others to Cambridge; we visited the Royal Academy and the Tate;* heard modern music in concert rooms, went to the Law Courts, and saw new plays. No one dined out without asking her partner certain questions and carefully noting his replies. At intervals we met together and compared our observations. Oh, those were merry meetings! Never have I laughed so much as I did when Rose read her notes upon 'Honour' and described how she had dressed herself as an Ethiopian Prince and gone aboard one of His Majesty's ships. Discovering the hoax, the Captain visited her (now disguised as a private gentleman) and demanded that honour should be satisfied. 'But how?' she asked. 'How?' he bellowed. 'With the cane of course!' Seeing that he was beside himself with rage and expecting that her last moment had come, she bent over and received to her amazement, six light taps upon the behind.* 'The honour of the British Navy is avenged!' he cried, and, raising herself, she saw him with the sweat pouring down his face holding out a trembling right hand. 'Away!' she exclaimed, striking an attitude and imitating the ferocity of his own expression, 'My honour has still to be satisfied!' 'Spoken like a gentleman!' he returned, and fell into profound thought. 'If six strokes avenge the honour of the King's Navy' he mused, 'how many avenge the honour of a private gentleman?' He said he would prefer to lay the case before his brother officers. She replied haughtily that she could not wait. He praised her sensibility. 'Let me see,' he cried suddenly, 'did your father keep a carriage?' 'No' she said. 'Or a riding horse?' 'We had a donkey,' she bethought her, 'which drew the mowing machine.' At this his face lightened. 'My mother's name—' she added. 'For God's sake, man, don't mention your mother's name!' he shrieked, trembling like an aspen and flushing to the roots of his hair, and it was ten minutes at least before she could induce him to proceed. At length he decreed that if she gave him four strokes and a half in the small of the back at a spot indicated by himself (the half conceded, he said, in recognition of the fact that her great grandmother's uncle was killed at Trafalgar*) it was his opinion that her honour would be as good as new. This was done; they retired to a restaurant; drank two bottles of wine for which he insisted upon paying; and parted with protestations of eternal friendship.

Then we had Fanny's account of her visit to the Law Courts.* At
her first visit she had come to the conclusion that the Judges were
either made of wood or were impersonated by large animals resembling man who had been trained to move with extreme dignity, mum-
ble and nod their heads. To test her theory she had liberated
a handkerchief of bluebottles at the critical moment of a trial, but was
unable to judge whether the creatures gave signs of humanity for the
buzzing of the flies induced so sound a sleep that she only woke in
time to see the prisoners led into the cells below. But from the
evidence she brought we voted that it is unfair to suppose that the
Judges are men.

Helen* went to the Royal Academy,* but when asked to deliver her
report upon the pictures she began to recite from a pale blue volume
'O for the touch of a vanished hand and the sound of a voice that is
still. Home is the hunter, home from the hill. He gave his bridle reins
a shake. Love is sweet, love is brief. Spring, the fair spring, is the
year's pleasant King. O! to be in England now that April's there. Men
must work and women must weep. The path of duty is the way to
glory—'* We could listen to no more of this gibberish.

'We want no more poetry!' we cried.

'Daughters of England!'* she began, but here we pulled her down,
a vase of water getting spilt over her in the scuffle.

'Thank God!' she exclaimed, shaking herself like a dog. 'Now I'll
roll on the carpet and see if I can't brush off what remains of the
Union Jack. Then perhaps—' here she rolled energetically. Getting
up she began to explain to us what modern pictures are like when
Castalia* stopped her.

'What is the average size of a picture?' she asked. 'Perhaps two feet
by two and a half,' she said. Castalia made notes while Helen spoke,
and when she had done, and we were trying not to meet each others
eyes, rose and said, 'At your wish I spent last week at Oxbridge, disguised as a charwoman. I thus had access to the rooms of several
Professors and will now attempt to give you some idea—only,' she
broke off, 'I can't think how to do it. It's all so queer. These Professors,'
she went on, 'live in large houses built round grass plots each in
a kind of cell by himself. Yet they have every convenience and comfort. You have only to press a button or light a little lamp. Their
papers are beautifully filed. Books abound. There are no children or
animals, save half a dozen stray cats and one aged bullfinch—a cock.

I remember,' she broke off, 'an Aunt of mine who lived at Dulwich*
and kept cactuses. You reached the conservatory through the double
drawing-room, and there, on the hot pipes, were dozens of them,
ugly, squat, bristly little plants each in a separate pot. Once in a hundred years the Aloe flowered,* so my Aunt said. But she died before
that happened—' We told her to keep to the point. 'Well,' she
resumed, 'when Professor Hobkin was out I examined his life work,
an edition of Sappho.* It's a queer looking book, six or seven inches
thick, not all by Sappho. Oh no. Most of it is a defence of Sappho's
chastity, which some German had denied, and I can assure you the
passion with which these two gentlemen argued, the learning they
displayed, the prodigious ingenuity with which they disputed the use
of some implement which looked to me for all the world like a hairpin
astounded me; especially when the door opened and Professor Hobkin
himself appeared. A very nice, mild, old gentleman, but what could *he*
know about chastity?' We misunderstood her.

'No, no,' she protested, 'he's the soul of honour I'm sure—not that
he resembles Rose's sea captain in the least. I was thinking rather of
my Aunt's cactuses. What could *they* know about chastity?'

Again we told her not to wander from the point,—did the Oxbridge
professors help to produce good people and good books?—the objects
of life.

'There!' she exclaimed. 'It never struck me to ask. It never occurred
to me that they could possibly produce anything.'

'I believe,' said Sue, 'that you made some mistake. Probably
Professor Hobkin was a gynaecologist. A scholar is a very different
sort of man. A scholar is overflowing with humour and invention—perhaps addicted to wine, but what of that?—a delightful companion, generous, subtle, imaginative—as stands to reason. For he
spends his life in company with the finest human beings that have
ever existed.'

'Hum,' said Castalia. 'Perhaps I'd better go back and try again.'

Some three months later it happened that I was sitting alone when
Castalia entered. I don't know what it was in the look of her that so
moved me; but I could not restrain myself, and dashing across the
room, I clasped her in my arms. Not only was she very beautiful; she
seemed also in the highest spirits. 'How happy you look!' I exclaimed,
as she sat down.

'I've been at Oxbridge' she said.

'Asking questions?'

'Answering them' she replied.

'You have not broken our vow?' I said anxiously, noticing something about her figure.

'Oh, the vow' she said casually. 'I'm going to have a baby if that's what you mean. You can't imagine,' she burst out, 'how exciting, how beautiful, how satisfying—'

'What is?' I asked.

'To—to—answer questions,' she replied in some confusion. Whereupon she told me the whole of her story. But in the middle of an account which interested and excited me more than anything I had ever heard, she gave the strangest cry, half whoop, half holloa—

'Chastity! Chastity! Where's my chastity!' she cried. 'Help Ho! The scent bottle!'

There was nothing in the room but a cruet containing mustard, which I was about to administer when she recovered her composure.

'You should have thought of that three months ago' I said severely.

'True' she replied. 'There's not much good in thinking of it now. It was unfortunate, by the way, that my mother had me called Castalia.'

'Oh Castalia, your mother—' I was beginning when she reached for the mustard pot.

'No, no, no,' she said, shaking her head. 'If you'd been a chaste woman yourself you would have screamed at the sight of me—instead of which you rushed across the room and took me in your arms. No, Cassandra.* We are neither of us chaste.' So we went on talking.

Meanwhile the room was filling up, for it was the day appointed to discuss the results of our observations. Everyone, I thought, felt as I did about Castalia. They kissed her and said how glad they were to see her again. At length, when we were all assembled, Jane rose and said that it was time to begin. She began by saying that we had now asked questions for over five years, and that though the results were bound to be inconclusive—here Castalia nudged me and whispered that she was not so sure about that. Then she got up, and, interrupting Jane in the middle of a sentence, said,

'Before you say any more, I want to know—am I to stay in the room? Because,' she added 'I have to confess that I am an impure woman.'

Everyone looked at her in astonishment.

'You are going to have a baby?' asked Jane.

She nodded her head.

It was extraordinary to see the different expressions on their faces. A sort of hum went through the room, in which I could catch the words 'impure,' 'baby,' 'Castalia,' and so on. Jane, who was herself considerably moved, put it to us,

'Shall she go? Is she impure?'

Such a roar filled the room as might have been heard in the street outside.

'No! No! No! Let her stay! Impure? Fiddlesticks!' Yet I fancied that some of the youngest, girls of nineteen or twenty, held back as if overcome with shyness. Then we all came about her and began asking questions, and at last I saw one of the youngest, who had kept in the background, approach shyly and say to her:

'What is chastity then? I mean is it good, or is it bad, or is it nothing at all?'* She replied so low that I could not catch what she said.

'You know I was shocked,' said another, 'for at least ten minutes.'

'In my opinion,' said Poll, who was growing crusty from always reading in the London Library, 'chastity is nothing but ignorance—a most discreditable state of mind. We should admit only the unchaste to our society. I vote that Castalia shall be our President.'

This was violently disputed.

'It is as unfair to brand women with chastity as with unchastity,' said Moll. 'Some of us haven't the opportunity either. Moreover, I don't believe Cassy herself maintains that she acted as she did from a pure love of knowledge.'

'He is only twenty one and divinely beautiful' said Cassy, with a ravishing gesture.

'I move,' said Helen, 'that no one be allowed to talk of chastity or unchastity save those who are in love.'

'Oh bother,' said Judith, who had been enquiring into scientific matters, 'I'm not in love and I'm longing to explain my measures for dispensing with prostitutes and fertilizing virgins by Act of Parliament.'

She went on to tell us of an invention of hers to be erected at Tube stations and other public resorts, which, upon payment of a small fee would safeguard the nation's health, accommodate its sons, and relieve its daughters. Then she had contrived a method of preserving in sealed tubes the germs of future Lord Chancellors 'or poets or painters or musicians' she went on, 'supposing, that is to say, that these breeds are not extinct, and that women still wish to bear children—'*

'Of course we wish to bear children!' cried Castalia impatiently. Jane rapped the table.

'That is the very point we are met to consider,' she said. 'For five years we have been trying to find out whether we are justified in continuing the human race. Castalia has anticipated our decision. But it remains for the rest of us to make up our minds.'

Here one after another of our messengers rose and delivered their reports. The marvels of civilization far exceeded our expectations, and as we learnt for the first time how man flies in the air, talks across space, penetrates to the heart of an atom, and embraces the universe in his speculations a murmur of admiration burst from our lips.

'We are proud,' we cried, 'that our mothers sacrificed their youth in such a cause as this!' Castalia, who had been listening intently, looked prouder than all the rest. Then Jane reminded us that we had still much to learn, and Castalia begged us to make haste. On we went through a vast tangle of statistics. We learnt that England has a population of so many millions, and that such and such a proportion of them is constantly hungry and in prison; that the average size of a working man's family is such, and that so great a percentage of women die from maladies incident to childbirth. Reports were read of visits to factories, shops, slums, and dockyards. Descriptions were given of the Stock Exchange, of a gigantic house of business in the City, and of a Government Office. The British Colonies were now discussed, and some account was given of our rule in India, Africa and Ireland. I was sitting by Castalia and I noticed her uneasiness.

'We shall never come to any conclusion at all at this rate,' she said. 'As it appears that civilization is so much more complex than we had any notion, would it not be better to confine ourselves to our original enquiry? We agreed that it was the object of life to produce good people and good books. All this time we have been talking of aeroplanes, factories and money. Let us talk about men themselves and their arts, for that is the heart of the matter.'

So the diners out stepped forward with long slips of paper containing answers to their questions. These had been framed after much consideration. A good man, we had agreed, must at any rate be honest, passionate, and unworldly. But whether or not a particular man possessed those qualities could only be discovered by asking questions, often beginning at a remote distance from the centre. Is Kensington* a nice place to live in? Where is your son being educated—and your daughter? Now please tell me, what do you pay for your cigars? By the way, is Sir Joseph a baronet or only a knight?* Often it seemed that we learnt more from trivial questions of this kind than from more direct ones. 'I accepted my peerage,' said Lord Bunkum* 'because my wife wished it.' I forget how many titles were accepted for the same reason. 'Working fifteen hours out of the twenty-four as I do—' ten thousand professional men began.

'No, no, of course you can neither read nor write. But why do you work so hard?' 'My dear lady, with a growing family—' 'but *why* does your family grow?' Their wives wished that too, or perhaps it was the British Empire. But more significant than the answers were the refusals to answer. Very few would reply at all to questions about morality and religion, and such answers as were given were not serious. Questions as to the value of money and power were almost invariably brushed aside, or pressed at extreme risk to the asker. 'I'm sure,' said Jill, 'that if Sir Harley Tightboots hadn't been carving the mutton when I asked him about the capitalist system he would have cut my throat. The only reason why we escaped with our lives over and over again is that men are at once so hungry and so chivalrous. They despise us too much to mind what we say.'

'Of course they despise us' said Eleanor. 'At the same time how do you account for this—I made enquiries among the artists. Now no woman has ever been an artist, has she, Poll?'

'Jane-Austen-Charlotte-Bronte-George-Eliot,' cried Poll, like a man crying muffins in a back street.

'Damn the woman!' someone exclaimed. 'What a bore she is!'

'Since Sappho there has been no female of first rate—' Eleanor began, quoting from a weekly newspaper.

'It's now well known that Sappho was the somewhat lewd invention of Professor Hobkin,' Ruth interrupted.

'Anyhow, there is no reason to suppose that any woman ever has been able to write or ever will be able to write' Eleanor continued. 'And yet, whenever I go among authors they never cease to talk to me about their books. Masterly! I say, or Shakespeare himself! (for one must say something) and I assure you, they believe me.'

'That proves nothing,' said Jane. They all do it. 'Only,' she sighed, 'It doesn't seem to help *us* much. Perhaps we had better examine modern literature next. Liz, it's your turn.'

Elizabeth rose and said that in order to prosecute her enquiry she had dressed as a man and been taken for a reviewer.

'I have read new books pretty steadily for the past five years,' said she. 'Mr Wells is the most popular living writer; then comes Mr Arnold Bennett; then Mr Compton Mackenzie; Mr McKenna and Mr Walpole* may be bracketed together.' She sat down.

'But you've told us nothing!' we expostulated. 'Or do you mean that these gentlemen have greatly surpassed Jane-Eliot and that English fiction is—where's that review of yours? Oh, yes, "safe in their hands." '

'Safe, quite safe' she said, shifting uneasily from foot to foot. 'And I'm sure that they give away even more than they receive.'

We were all sure of that. 'But,' we pressed her, 'do they write good books?'

'Good books?' she said, looking at the ceiling. 'You must remember,' she began, speaking with extreme rapidity, 'that fiction is the mirror of life. And you can't deny that education is of the highest importance, and that it would be extremely annoying, if you found yourself alone at Brighton late at night, not to know which was the best boarding house to stay at, and suppose it was a dripping Sunday evening—wouldn't it be nice to go to the Movies?'

'But what has that got to do with it?' we asked.

'Nothing—nothing—nothing whatever' she replied.

'Well, tell us the truth' we bade her.

'The truth? But isn't it wonderful,' she broke off—'Mr Chitter has written a weekly article for the past thirty years upon love or hot buttered toast and has sent all his sons to Eton—'

'The truth!' we demanded.

'Oh the truth,' she stammered—'the truth has nothing to do with literature,' and sitting down she refused to say another word.

It all seemed to us very inconclusive.

'Ladies, we must try to sum up the results' Jane was beginning, when a hum, which had been heard for some time through the open window, drowned her voice.

'War! War! War! Declaration of War!'* men were shouting in the street below.

We looked at each other in horror.

'What war?' we cried. 'What war?' We remembered, too late, that we had never thought of sending anyone to the House of Commons.

We had forgotten all about it. We turned to Poll, who had reached the history shelves in the London Library, and asked her to enlighten us.

'Why,' we cried 'do men go to war?'

'Sometimes for one reason, sometimes for another' she replied calmly. 'In 1760, for example—' The shouts outside drowned her words. 'Again in 1797—in 1804—It was the Austrians in 1866—1870 was the Franco-Prussian—In 1900 on the other hand—'*

'But it's now 1914!' we cut her short.

'Ah, I don't know what they're going to war for now,' she admitted.

* * *

The war was over and peace was in process of being signed when I once more found myself with Castalia in the room where our meetings used to be held. We began idly turning over the pages of our old minute books. 'Queer,' I mused, 'to see what we were thinking five years ago.' 'We are agreed,' Castalia quoted, reading over my shoulder, 'that it is the object to life to produce good people and good books.' We made no comment upon that. 'A good man is at any rate honest passionate and unworldly.' 'What a woman's language' I observed. 'Oh dear,' cried Castalia, pushing the book away from her, 'What fools we were! It was all Poll's father's fault,' she went on. 'I believe he did it on purpose—that ridiculous will, I mean, forcing Poll to read all the books in the London Library. If we hadn't learnt to read,' she said bitterly, 'we might still have been bearing children in ignorance and that I believe was the happiest life after all. I know what you're going to say about war,' she checked me, 'and the horror of bearing children to see them killed, but our mothers did it, and their mothers, and their mothers before them. And *they* didn't complain. They couldn't read. I've done my best,' she sighed, 'to prevent my little girl from learning to read, but what's the use? I caught Ann only yesterday with a newspaper in her hand and she was beginning to ask me if it was "true". Next she'll ask me whether Mr Lloyd George* is a good man, then whether Mr Arnold Bennett is a good novelist, and finally whether I believe in God. How can I bring my daughter up to believe in nothing?' she demanded.

'Surely you could teach her to believe that a man's intellect is, and always will be, fundamentally superior to a woman's?' I suggested. She brightened at this and began to turn over our old minutes again. 'Yes,' she said, 'think of their discoveries, their mathematics, their science, their philosophy, their scholarship—' and then she began to laugh, 'I shall never forget old Hobkin and the hairpin,' she said, and went on reading and laughing and I thought she was quite happy, when suddenly she threw the book from her and burst out, 'Oh, Cassandra why do you torment me? Don't you know that our belief in man's intellect is the greatest fallacy of them all?' 'What?' I exclaimed. 'Ask any journalist, schoolmaster, politician or public house keeper in the land and they will all tell you that men are much cleverer than women.' 'As if I doubted it,' she said scornfully. 'How could they help it? Haven't we bred them and fed and kept them in comfort since the beginning of time so that they may be clever even if they're nothing else? It's all our doing!'* she cried. 'We insisted upon having intellect and now we've got it. And it's intellect,' she continued, 'that's at the bottom of it. What could be more charming than a boy before he has begun to cultivate his intellect? He is beautiful to look at; he gives himself no airs; he understands the meaning of art and literature instinctively; he goes about enjoying his life and making other people enjoy theirs. Then they teach him to cultivate his intellect. He becomes a barrister, a civil servant, a general, an author, a professor. Every day he goes to an office. Every year he produces a book. He maintains a whole family by the products of his brain—poor devil! Soon he cannot come into a room without making us all feel uncomfortable; he condescends to every woman he meets, and dares not tell the truth even to his own wife; instead of rejoicing our eyes we have to shut them if we are to take him in our arms. True, they console themselves with stars of all shapes, ribbons of all shades, and incomes of all sizes—but what is to console us? That we shall be able in ten years' time to spend a weekend at Lahore? Or that the least insect in Japan has a name twice the length of its body? Oh, Cassandra, for Heaven's sake let us devise a method by which men may bear children! It is our only chance. For unless we provide them with some innocent occupation we shall get neither good people nor good books; we shall perish beneath the fruits of their unbridled activity; and not a human being will survive to know that there once was Shakespeare!'

'It is too late,' I said. 'We cannot provide even for the children that we have.'

'And then you ask me to believe in intellect,' she said.

While we spoke, men were crying hoarsely and wearily in the street, and listening, we heard that the Treaty of Peace had just been signed.*

The voices died away. The rain was falling and interfered no doubt with the proper explosion of the fireworks.

'My cook will have bought the *Evening News*'* said Castalia 'and Ann will be spelling it out over her tea. I must go home.'

'It's no good—not a bit of good' I said. 'Once she knows how to read there's only one thing you can teach her to believe in—and that is herself.'

'Well, that would be a change,' said Castalia.

So we swept up the papers of our Society, and though Ann was playing with her doll very happily, we solemnly made her a present of the lot and told her we had chosen her to be President of the Society of the future—upon which she burst into tears, poor little girl.

IN THE ORCHARD

MIRANDA slept in the orchard, lying in a long chair beneath the apple tree. Her book had fallen into the grass, and her finger still seemed to point at the sentence '*Ce pays est vraiment un des coins du monde où le rire des filles éclate le mieux . . .*'* as if she had fallen asleep just there. The opals on her finger flushed green, flushed rosy, and again flushed orange as the sun, oozing through the apple trees, filled them. Then, when the breeze blew, her purple dress rippled like a flower attached to a stalk; the grasses nodded; and the white butterfly came blowing this way and that just above her face.

Four feet in the air over her head the apples hung. Suddenly there was a shrill clamour as if they were gongs of cracked brass beaten violently, irregularly, and brutally. It was only the school-children saying the multiplication table in unison, stopped by the teacher, scolded, and beginning to say the multiplication table over again. But this clamour passed four feet above Miranda's head, went through the apple boughs, and, striking against the cowman's little boy who was picking blackberries in the hedge when he should have been at school, made him tear his thumb on the thorns.

Next there was a solitary cry—sad, human, brutal. Old Parsley was, indeed, blind drunk.

Then the very topmost leaves of the apple tree, flat like little fish against the blue, thirty feet above the earth, chimed with a pensive and lugubrious note. It was the organ in the church playing one of Hymns Ancient and Modern.* The sound floated out and was cut into atoms by a flock of fieldfares flying at an enormous speed—somewhere or other. Miranda lay asleep thirty feet beneath.

Then above the apple tree and the pear tree two hundred feet above Miranda lying asleep in the orchard bells thudded, intermittent, sullen, didactic, for six poor women of the parish were being churched* and the Rector was returning thanks to heaven.

And above that with a sharp squeak the golden feather of the church tower* turned from south to east. The wind changed. Above everything else it droned, above the woods, the meadows, the hills, miles above Miranda lying in the orchard asleep. It swept on, eyeless, brainless, meeting nothing that could stand against it, until, wheeling the other way, it turned south again. Miles below, in a space as big as the eye of a needle, Miranda stood upright and cried aloud: 'Oh, I shall be late for tea!'

Miranda slept in the orchard—or perhaps she was not asleep, for her lips moved very slightly as if they were saying, '*Ce pays est vraiment un des coins du monde . . . où le rire des filles . . . éclate . . . éclate . . . éclate . . .*' and then she smiled and let her body sink all its weight on to the enormous earth which rises, she thought, to carry me on its back as if I were a leaf, or a queen (here the children said the multiplication table), or, Miranda went on, I might be lying on the top of a cliff with the gulls screaming above me. The higher they fly, she continued, as the teacher scolded the children and rapped Jimmy over the knuckles till they bled, the deeper they look into the sea—into the sea, she repeated, and her fingers relaxed and her lips closed gently as if she were floating on the sea, and then, when the shout of the drunken man sounded overhead, she drew breath with an extraordinary ecstasy, for she thought that she heard life itself crying out from a rough tongue in a scarlet mouth, from the wind, from the bells, from the curved green leaves of the cabbages.

Naturally she was being married when the organ played the tune from Hymns Ancient and Modern, and, when the bells rang after the six poor women had been churched, the sullen intermittent thud made her think that the very earth shook with the hoofs of the horse that was galloping towards her ('Ah, I have only to wait!' she sighed), and it seemed to her that everything had already begun moving, crying, riding, flying round her, across her, towards her in a pattern.

Mary is chopping the wood, she thought; Pearman is herding the cows; the carts are coming up from the meadows; the rider—and she traced out the lines that the men, the carts, the birds, and the rider made over the countryside until they all seemed driven out, round, and across by the beat of her own heart.

Miles up in the air the wind changed; the golden feather of the church tower squeaked; and Miranda jumped up and cried: 'Oh, I shall be late for tea!'

Miranda slept in the orchard, or was she asleep or was she not asleep? Her purple dress stretched between the two apple trees. There were twenty-four apple trees in the orchard, some slanting slightly, others growing straight with a rush up the trunk which spread wide into branches and formed into round red or yellow drops. Each apple tree had sufficient space. The sky exactly fitted the leaves. When the breeze blew, the line of the boughs against the wall slanted slightly and then returned. A wagtail flew diagonally from one corner to another. Cautiously hopping, a thrush advanced towards a fallen apple; from the other wall a sparrow fluttered just above the grass. The uprush of the trees was tied down by these movements; the whole was compacted by the orchard walls. For miles beneath the earth was clamped together; rippled on the surface with wavering air; and across the corner of the orchard the blue-green was slit by a purple streak. The wind changing, one bunch of apples was tossed so high that it blotted out two cows in the meadow ('Oh, I shall be late for tea!' cried Miranda), and the apples hung straight across the wall again.

A WOMAN'S COLLEGE FROM OUTSIDE

THE feathery-white moon never let the sky grow dark; all night the chestnut blossoms were white in the green, and dim was the cow-parsley in the meadows.* Neither to Tartary* nor to Arabia went the wind of the Cambridge courts, but lapsed dreamily in the midst of grey-blue clouds over the roofs of Newnham.* There, in the garden, if she needed space to wander, she might find it among the trees; and as none but women's faces could meet her face, she might unveil it, blank, featureless, and gaze into rooms where at that hour, blank, featureless, eyelids white over eyes, ringless hands extended upon sheets, slept innumerable women. But here and there a light still burned.

A double light one might figure in Angela's room, seeing how bright Angela herself was, and how bright came back the reflection of herself from the square glass. The whole of her was perfectly delineated—perhaps the soul. For the glass held up an untrembling image—white and gold, red slippers, pale hair with blue stones in it, and never a ripple or shadow to break the smooth kiss of Angela and her reflection in the glass, as if she were glad to be Angela. Anyhow the moment was glad—the bright picture hung in the heart of night, the shrine hollowed in the nocturnal blackness. Strange indeed to have this visible proof of the rightness of things; this lily floating flawless upon Time's pool, fearless, as if this were sufficient—this reflection. Which meditation she betrayed by turning, and the mirror held nothing at all, or only the brass bedstead, and she, running here and there, patting and darting, became like a woman in a house, and changed again, pursing her lips over a black book and marking with her finger what surely could not be a firm grasp of the science of economics. Only Angela Williams was at Newnham for the purpose of earning her living, and could not forget even in moments of impassioned adoration the cheques of her father at Swansea: her mother washing in the scullery: pink frocks out to dry on the line; tokens that even the lily no longer floats flawless upon the pool, but has a name on a card like another.

A. Williams—one may read it in the moonlight; and next to it some Mary or Eleanor, Mildred, Sarah, Phoebe upon square cards on their doors. All names, nothing but names. The cool white light withered them and starched them until it seemed as if the only purpose of all these names was to rise martially in order should there be a call on them to extinguish a fire, suppress an insurrection, or pass an examination. Such is the power of names written upon cards pinned upon doors. Such too the resemblance, what with tiles, corridors, and bedroom doors, to dairy or nunnery, a place of seclusion or discipline, where the bowl of milk stands cool and pure and there's a great washing of linen.

At that very moment soft laughter came from behind a door. A prim-voiced clock struck the hour—one, two. Now if the clock were issuing his commands, they were disregarded. Fire, insurrection, examination, were all snowed under by laughter, or softly uprooted, the sound seeming to bubble up from the depths and gently waft away the hour, rules, discipline. The bed was strewn with cards. Sally was on the floor. Helena in the chair. Good Bertha clasping her hands by the fire-place. A. Williams came in yawning.

'Because it's utterly and intolerably damnable,' said Helena.

'Damnable,' echoed Bertha. Then yawned.

'We're not eunuchs.'

'I saw her slipping in by the back gate with that old hat on. They don't want us to know.'

'They?' said Angela. 'She.'

Then the laughter.

The cards were spread, falling with their red and yellow faces on the table, and hands were dabbled in the cards. Good Bertha, leaning with her head against the chair, sighed profoundly. For she would willingly have slept, but since night is free pasturage, a limitless field, since night is unmoulded richness, one must tunnel into its darkness. One must hang it with jewels. Night was shared in secret, day browsed on by the whole flock. The blinds were up. A mist was on the garden. Sitting on the floor by the window (while the others played), body, mind, both together, seemed blown through the air, to trail across the bushes. Ah, but she desired to stretch out in bed and to sleep! She believed that no one felt her desire for sleep; she believed humbly—sleepily—with sudden nods and lurchings, that other people were wide awake. When they laughed all together a bird chirped in its sleep out in the garden, as if the laughter—

Yes, as if the laughter (for she dozed now) floated out much like mist and attached itself by soft elastic shreds to plants and bushes, so that the garden was vaporous and clouded. And then, swept by the wind, the bushes would bow themselves and the white vapours blow off across the world.

From all the rooms where women slept this vapour issued, attaching itself to shrubs, like mist, and then blew freely out into the open. Elderly women slept, who would on waking immediately clasp the ivory rod of office. Now smooth and colourless, reposing deeply, they lay surrounded, lay supported, by the bodies of youth recumbent or grouped at the window; pouring forth into the garden this bubbling laughter, this irresponsible laughter: this laughter of mind and body floating away rules, hours, discipline: immensely fertilizing, yet formless, chaotic, trailing and straying and tufting the rose-bushes with shreds of vapour.

'Ah,' breathed Angela, standing at the window in her night-gown. Pain was in her voice. She leant her head out. The mist was cleft as if her voice parted it. She had been talking, while the others played, to Alice Avery, about Bamborough Castle,* the colour of the sands at evening, upon which Alice said she would write and settle the day, in August, and stooping, kissed her, at least touched her head with her hand, and Angela, positively unable to sit still, like one possessed of a wind-lashed sea in her heart, roamed up and down the room (the witness of such a scene) throwing her arms out to relieve this excitement, this astonishment at the incredible stooping of the miraculous tree with the golden fruit at its summit—hadn't it dropped into her arms? She held it glowing to her breast, a thing not to be touched, thought of, or spoken about, but left to glow there. And then, slowly putting there her stockings, there her slippers, folding her petticoat neatly on top, Angela, her other name being Williams, realized—how could she express it?—that after the dark churning of myriad ages here was light at the end of the tunnel; life; the world. Beneath her it lay—all good; all lovable. Such was her discovery.

Indeed, how could one then feel surprise if, lying in bed, she could not close her eyes?—something irresistibly unclosed them—if in the shallow darkness chair and chest of drawers looked stately, and the looking-glass precious with its ashen hint of day? Sucking her thumb like a child (her age nineteen last November), she lay in this good world, this new world, this world at the end of the tunnel, until a desire to see it or forestall it drove her, tossing her blankets, to guide herself to the window, and there, looking out upon the garden, where the mist lay, all the windows open, one fiery-bluish, something murmuring in the distance, the world of course, and the morning coming, 'Oh,' she cried, as if in pain.

THE NEW DRESS

MABEL had her first serious suspicion that something was wrong as she took her cloak off and Mrs Barnet, while handing her the mirror and touching the brushes and thus drawing her attention, perhaps rather markedly, to all the appliances for tidying and improving hair, complexion, clothes, which existed on the dressing table, confirmed the suspicion,—that it was not right, not quite right, which growing stronger as she went upstairs and springing at her with conviction as she greeted Clarissa Dalloway, she went straight to the far end of the room, to a shaded corner where a looking-glass hung and looked. No! It was not right. And at once the misery which she always tried to hide, the profound dissatisfaction,—the sense she had had, ever since she was a child, of being inferior to other people,—set upon her, relentlessly, remorselessly, with an intensity which she could not beat off, as she would when she woke at night at home, by reading Borrow or Scott;* for oh these men, oh these women, all were thinking,— 'What's Mabel wearing? What a fright she looks! What a hideous new dress!'—their eyelids flickering as they came up and then their lids shutting rather tight. It was her own appalling inadequacy; her cowardice; her mean, water-sprinkled blood that depressed her. And at once the whole of the room where, for ever so many hours, she had planned with the little dressmaker how it was to go, seemed sordid, repulsive; and her own drawing-room so shabby, and herself, going out, puffed up with vanity as she touched the letters on the hall table and said: 'How dull!' to show off,—all this now seemed unutterably silly, paltry, and provincial. All this had been absolutely destroyed, shown up, exploded, the moment she came into Mrs Dalloway's drawing-room.

What she had thought that evening when, sitting over the tea-cups, Mrs Dalloway's invitation came, was that, of course, she could not be fashionable. It was absurd to pretend it even,—fashion meant cut, meant style, meant thirty guineas at least,—but why not be original? Why not be herself, anyhow? And, getting up, she had taken that old fashion book of her mother's, a Paris fashion book of the time of the Empire,* and had thought how much prettier, more dignified, and more womanly they were then, and so set herself,—oh, it was foolish,—trying to be like them, pluming herself in fact, upon being modest and old-fashioned and very charming, giving herself up, no doubt about it, to an orgy of self-love, which deserved to be chastised, and so rigged herself out like this.

But she dared not look in the glass. She could not face the whole horror,—the pale yellow, idiotically old-fashioned silk dress with its long skirt and its high sleeves and its waist and all the things that looked so charming in the fashion book, but not on her, not among all these ordinary people. She felt like a dress-maker's dummy standing there, for young people to stick pins into.

'But, my dear, it's perfectly charming!' Rose Shaw said, looking her up and down with that little satirical pucker of the lips which she expected,—Rose herself being dressed in the height of the fashion, precisely like everybody else, always.

We are all like flies trying to crawl over the edge of the saucer, Mabel thought, and repeated the phrase as if she were crossing herself, as if she were trying to find some spell to annul this pain, to make this agony endurable. Tags of Shakespeare, lines from books she had read ages ago, suddenly came to her when she was in agony, and she repeated them over and over again. 'Flies trying to crawl,' she repeated.* If she could say that over often enough and make herself see the flies, she would become numb, chill, frozen, dumb. Now she could see flies crawling slowly out of a saucer of milk with their wings stuck together; and she strained and strained (standing in front of the looking-glass, listening to Rose Shaw) to make herself see Rose Shaw and all the other people there as flies, trying to hoist themselves out of something, or into something, meagre, insignificant, toiling flies. But she could not see them like that, not other people. She saw herself like that,—she was a fly, but the others were dragon-flies, butterflies, beautiful insects, dancing, fluttering, skimming, while she alone dragged herself up out of the saucer. (Envy and spite, the most detestable of the vices, were her chief faults.)

'I feel like some dowdy, decrepit, horribly dingy old fly,' she said, making Robert Haydon stop just to hear her say that, just to reassure herself by furbishing up a poor weak-kneed phrase and so showing how detached she was, how witty, that she did not feel in the least out of anything. And, of course, Robert Haydon answered something quite polite, quite insincere, which she saw through instantly, and said to herself, directly he went, (again from some book), 'Lies, lies, lies!'* For a party makes things either much more real, or much less real, she thought; she saw in a flash to the bottom of Robert Haydon's heart; she saw through everything. She saw the truth. This was true, this drawing-room, this self, and the other false. Miss Milan's little workroom was really terribly hot, stuffy, sordid. It smelt of clothes and cabbage cooking; and yet, when Miss Milan put the glass in her hand, and she looked at herself with the dress on, finished, an extraordinary bliss shot through her heart. Suffused with light, she sprang into existence. Rid of cares and wrinkles, what she had dreamed of herself was there,—a beautiful woman. Just for a second (she had not dared look longer, Miss Milan wanted to know about the length of the skirt), there looked at her, framed in the scrolloping* mahogany, a gray-white, mysteriously smiling, charming girl, the core of herself, the soul of herself; and it was not vanity only, not only self-love that made her think it good, tender, and true. Miss Milan said that the skirt could not well be longer; if anything the skirt, said Miss Milan, puckering her forehead, considering with all her wits about her, must be shorter; and she felt, suddenly, honestly, full of love for Miss Milan, much, much fonder of Miss Milan than of any one in the whole world, and could have cried for pity that she should be crawling on the floor with her mouth full of pins, and her face red and her eyes bulging,—that one human being should be doing this for another, and she saw them all as human beings merely, and herself going off to her party, and Miss Milan pulling the cover over the canary's cage, or letting him pick a hemp-seed from between her lips, and the thought of it, of this side of human nature and its patience and its endurance and its being content with such miserable, scanty, sordid, little pleasures filled her eyes with tears.

And now the whole thing had vanished. The dress, the room, the love, the pity, the scrolloping looking-glass, and the canary's cage,—all had vanished, and here she was in a corner of Mrs Dalloway's drawing-room, suffering tortures, woken wide awake to reality.

But it was all so paltry, weak-blooded, and petty-minded to care so much at her age with two children, to be still so utterly dependent on people's opinions and not have principles or convictions, not to be able to say as other people did, 'There's Shakespeare! There's death! We're all weevils in a captain's biscuit,'—or whatever it was that people did say.

She faced herself straight in the glass; she pecked at her left shoulder; she issued out into the room, as if spears were thrown at her yellow dress from all sides. But instead of looking fierce or tragic, as Rose Shaw would have done,—Rose would have looked like Boadicea,*—she looked foolish and self-conscious, and simpered like a schoolgirl and slouched across the room, positively slinking, as if she were a beaten mongrel, and looked at a picture, an engraving. As if one went to a party to look at a picture! Everybody knew why she did it,—it was from shame, from humiliation.

'Now the fly's in the saucer,' she said to herself, 'right in the middle, and can't get out, and the milk,' she thought, rigidly staring at the picture, 'is sticking its wings together.'

'It's so old-fashioned,' she said to Charles Burt, making him stop (which by itself he hated) on his way to talk to some one else.

She meant, or she tried to make herself think that she meant, that it was the picture and not her dress, that was old-fashioned. And one word of praise, one word of affection from Charles would have made all the difference to her at the moment. If he had only said, 'Mabel, you're looking charming to-night!' it would have changed her life. But then she ought to have been truthful and direct. Charles said nothing of the kind, of course. He was malice itself. He always saw through one, especially if one were feeling particularly mean, paltry, or feeble-minded.

'Mabel's got a new dress!' he said, and the poor fly was absolutely shoved into the middle of the saucer. Really, he would like her to drown, she believed. He had no heart, no fundamental kindness, only a veneer of friendliness. Miss Milan was much more real, much kinder. If only one could feel that and stick to it, always. 'Why,' she asked herself,—replying to Charles much too pertly, letting him see that she was out of temper, or 'ruffled' as he called it ('Rather ruffled?' he said and went on to laugh at her with some woman over there),—'Why,' she asked herself, 'can't I feel one thing always, feel quite sure that Miss Milan is right, and Charles wrong and stick to it, feel sure about the canary and pity and love and not be whipped all round in a second by coming into a room full of people?' It was her odious, weak, vacillating character again, always giving at the critical moment and not being seriously interested in conchology, etymology, botany, archeology, cutting up potatoes and watching them fructify like Mary Dennis, like Violet Searle.

Then Mrs Holman, seeing her standing there, bore down upon her. Of course a thing like a dress was beneath Mrs Holman's notice, with her family always tumbling downstairs or having the scarlet fever. Could Mabel tell her if Elmthorpe was ever let for August and September? Oh, it was a conversation that bored her unutterably!—it made her furious to be treated like a house agent or a messenger boy, to be made use of. Not to have value, that was it, she thought, trying to grasp something hard, something real, while she tried to answer sensibly about the bathroom and the south aspect and the hot water to the top of the house; and all the time she could see little bits of her yellow dress in the round looking-glass which made them all the size of boot-buttons or tadpoles; and it was amazing to think how much humiliation and agony and self-loathing and effort and passionate ups and downs of feeling were contained in a thing the size of a three penny bit.* And what was still odder, this thing, this Mabel Waring, was separate, quite disconnected; and though Mrs Holman (the black button) was leaning forward and telling her how her eldest boy had strained his heart running, she could see her, too, quite detached in the looking-glass, and it was impossible that the black dot, leaning forward, gesticulating, should make the yellow dot, sitting solitary, self-centred, feel what the black dot was feeling, yet they pretended.

'So impossible to keep boys quiet,'—that was the kind of thing one said.

And Mrs Holman, who could never get enough sympathy and snatched what little there was greedily, as if it were her right (but she deserved much more for there was her little girl who had come down this morning with a swollen knee-joint), took this miserable offering and looked at it suspiciously, grudgingly, as if it were a halfpenny when it ought to have been a pound and put it away in her purse, must put up with it, mean and miserly though it was, times being hard, so very hard; and on she went, creaking, injured Mrs Holman, about the girl with the swollen joints. Ah, it was tragic, this greed, this clamour of human beings, like a row of cormorants, barking and flapping their wings for sympathy,—it was tragic, could one have felt it and not merely pretended to feel it!

But in her yellow dress to-night she could not wring out one drop more; she wanted it all, all for herself. She knew (she kept on looking into the glass, dipping into that dreadfully showing-up blue pool) that she was condemned, despised, left like this in a backwater, because of her being like this a feeble, vacillating creature; and it seemed to her that the yellow dress was a penance which she had deserved, and if she had been dressed like Rose Shaw, in lovely, clinging green with a ruffle of swansdown, she would have deserved that; and she thought that there was no escape for her,—none whatever. But it was not her fault altogether, after all. It was being one of a family of ten; never having money enough, always skimping and paring; and her mother carrying great cans, and the linoleum worn on the stair edges, and one sordid little domestic tragedy after another,—nothing catastrophic, the sheep farm failing, but not utterly; her eldest brother marrying beneath him but not very much,—there was no romance, nothing extreme about them all. They petered out respectably in seaside resorts; every watering-place had one of her aunts even now asleep in some lodging with the front windows not quite facing the sea. That was so like them,—they had to squint at things always. And she had done the same,—she was just like her aunts. For all her dreams of living in India, married to some hero like Sir Henry Lawrence,* some empire builder (still the sight of a native in a turban filled her with romance), she had failed utterly. She had married Hubert, with his safe, permanent underling's job in the Law Courts, and they managed tolerably in a smallish house, without proper maids, and hash when she was alone or just bread and butter, but now and then,— Mrs Holman was off, thinking her the most dried-up, unsympathetic twig she had ever met, absurdly dressed, too, and would tell every one about Mabel's fantastic appearance,—now and then, thought Mabel Waring, left alone on the blue sofa, punching the cushion in order to look occupied, for she would not join Charles Burt and Rose Shaw, chattering like magpies and perhaps laughing at her by the fireplace,— now and then, there did come to her delicious moments, reading the other night in bed, for instance, or down by the sea on the sand in the sun, at Easter,—let her recall it,—a great tuft of pale sand-grass standing all twisted like a shock of spears against the sky, which was blue like a smooth china egg, so firm, so hard, and then the melody of the waves,—'Hush, hush,' they said, and the children's shouts paddling,—yes, it was a divine moment, and there she lay, she felt, in the hand of the Goddess who was the world; rather a hard-hearted, but very beautiful Goddess, a little lamb laid on the altar (one did think these silly things, and it didn't matter so long as one never said them). And also with Hubert sometimes she had quite unexpectedly,—carving the mutton for Sunday lunch, for no reason, opening a letter, coming into a room,—divine moments, when she said to herself (for she would never say this to anybody else), 'This is it. This has happened. This is it!' And the other way about it was equally surprising,—that is, when everything was arranged,—music, weather, holidays, every reason for happiness was there,—then nothing happened at all. One wasn't happy. It was flat, just flat, that was all.

Her wretched self again, no doubt! She had always been a fretful, weak, unsatisfactory mother, a wobbly wife, lolling about in a kind of twilight existence with nothing very clear or very bold or more one thing than another, like all her brothers and sisters, except perhaps Herbert,—they were all the same poor water-veined creatures who did nothing. Then in the midst of this creeping, crawling life, suddenly she was on the crest of a wave. That wretched fly,—where had she read the story that kept coming into her mind about the fly and the saucer?—struggled out. Yes, she had those moments. But now that she was forty, they might come more and more seldom. By degrees she would cease to struggle any more. But that was deplorable! That was not to be endured! That made her feel ashamed of herself!

She would go to the London Library to-morrow. She would find some wonderful, helpful, astonishing book, quite by chance, a book by a clergyman, by an American no one had ever heard of; or she would walk down the Strand* and drop, accidentally, into a hall where a miner was telling about the life in the pit and suddenly she would become a new person. She would be absolutely transformed. She would wear a uniform; she would be called Sister Somebody; she would never give a thought to clothes again. And for ever after she would be perfectly clear about Charles Burt and Miss Milan and this room and that room; and it would be always, day after day, as if she were lying in the sun or carving the mutton. It would be it!

So she got up from the blue sofa, and the yellow button in the looking-glass got up too, and she waved her hand to Charles and Rose to show them she did not depend on them one scrap, and the yellow button moved out of the looking-glass, and all the spears were gathered into her breast as she walked towards Mrs Dalloway and said, 'Good night.'

'But it's too early to go,' said Mrs Dalloway, who was always so charming.

'I'm afraid I must,' said Mabel Waring. 'But,' she added in her weak, wobbly voice which only sounded ridiculous when she tried to strengthen it, 'I have enjoyed myself enormously.'

'I have enjoyed myself,' she said to Mr Dalloway, whom she met on the stairs.

'Lies, lies, lies!' she said to herself, going downstairs, and 'Right in the saucer!' she said to herself as she thanked Mrs Barnet for helping her and wrapped herself, round and round and round, in the Chinese cloak she had worn these twenty years.

'SLATER'S PINS HAVE NO POINTS'*

'SLATER'S pins have no points—don't you always find that?' said Miss Craye, turning round as the rose fell out of Fanny Wilmot's dress, and Fanny stooped with her ears full of the music, to look for the pin on the floor.

The words gave her an extraordinary shock, as Miss Craye struck the last chord of the Bach fugue.* Did Miss Craye actually go to Slater's and buy pins then, Fanny Wilmot asked herself, transfixed for a moment? Did she stand at the counter waiting like anybody else, and was she given a bill with coppers wrapped in it, and did she slip them into her purse and then, an hour later, stand by her dressing table and take out the pins? What need had she of pins? For she was not so much dressed as cased, like a beetle compactly in its sheath, blue in winter, green in summer. What need had she of pins—Julia Craye?—who lived, it seemed, in the cool, glassy world of Bach fugues, playing to herself what she liked and only consenting to take one or two pupils at the Archer Street College of Music* (so the Principal, Miss Kingston said) as a special favour to herself, who had 'the greatest admiration for her in every way.' Miss Craye was left badly off, Miss Kingston was afraid, at her brother's death. Oh, they used to have such lovely things when they lived at Salisbury* and her brother Julius was, of course, a very well known man, a famous archæologist. It was a great privilege to stay with them, Miss Kingston said ('my family had always known them—they were regular Salisbury people,' Miss Kingston said) but a little frightening for a child; one had to be careful not to slam the door or bounce into the room unexpectedly. Miss Kingston, who gave little character sketches like this on the first day of term while she received cheques and wrote out receipts for them, smiled here. Yes, she had been rather a tomboy; she had bounced in and set all those green Roman glasses and things jumping in their case. The Crayes were none of them married. The Crayes were not used to children. They kept cats. The cats, one used to feel, knew as much about the Roman urns and things as anybody.

'Far more than I did!' said Miss Kingston brightly, writing her name across the stamp, in her dashing, cheerful, full bodied hand, for she had always been practical.

Perhaps then, Fanny Wilmot thought, looking for the pin, Miss Craye said that about 'Slater's pins having no points,' at a venture. None of the Crayes had ever married. She knew nothing about pins—nothing whatever. But she wanted to break the spell that had fallen on the house; to break the pane of glass which separated them from other people. When Polly Kingston, that merry little girl, had slammed the door and made the Roman vases jump, Julius, seeing that no harm was done (that would be his first instinct) looked, for the case was stood in the window, at Polly skipping home across the fields; looked with the look his sister often had, a lingering, desiring look.

'Stars, sun, moon,' it seemed to say, 'the daisy in the grass, fires, frost on the windowpane, my heart goes out to you. But,' it always seemed to add, 'you break, you pass, you go.' And simultaneously it covered the intensity of both these states of mind with 'I can't reach you—I can't get at you,' spoken wistfully, frustratedly. And the stars faded, and the child went.

That was the kind of spell, that was the glassy surface that Miss Craye wanted to break by showing, when she had played Bach beautifully as a reward to a favourite pupil (Fanny Wilmot knew that she was Miss Craye's favourite pupil) that she too felt as other people felt about pins. Slater's pins had no points.

Yes, the 'famous archæologist' had looked like that, too. 'The famous archæologist'—as she said that endorsing cheques, ascertaining the day of the month, speaking so briefly and frankly, there was in Miss Kingston's voice an indescribable tone which hinted at something odd, something queer, in Julius Craye. It was the very same thing that was odd perhaps in Julia, too. One could have sworn, thought Fanny Wilmot, as she looked for the pin, that at parties, meetings (Miss Kingston's father was a clergyman) she had picked up some piece of gossip, or it might only have been a smile, or a tone when his name was mentioned, which had given her 'a feeling' about Julius Craye. Needless to say, she had never spoken about it to anybody. Probably she scarcely knew what she meant by it. But whenever she spoke of Julius, or heard him mentioned, that was the first thought that came to mind: there was something odd about Julius Craye.

It was so that Julia looked too, as she sat half turned on the music stool, smiling. It's on the field, it's on the pane, it's in the sky—beauty; and I can't get at it; I can't have it—I, she seemed to add, with that little clutch of the hand which was so characteristic, who adore it so passionately, would give the whole world to possess it! And she picked up the carnation which had fallen on the floor, while Fanny searched for the pin. She crushed it, Fanny felt, voluptuously in her smooth, veined hands stuck about with water-coloured rings set in pearls. The pressure of her fingers seemed to increase all that was most brilliant in the flower; to set it off; to make it more frilled, fresh, immaculate. What was odd in her, and perhaps in her brother too, was that this crush and grasp of the fingers was combined with a perpetual frustration. So it was even now with the carnation. She had her hands on it; she pressed it; but she did not possess it, enjoy it, not altogether.

None of the Crayes had married, Fanny Wilmot remembered. She had in mind how one evening when the lesson had lasted longer than usual and it was dark, Julia Craye had said, 'It's the use of men, surely, to protect us,' smiling at her that same odd smile, as she stood fastening her cloak, which made her, like the flower, conscious to her finger tips of youth and brilliance, but like the flower too, Fanny suspected, inhibited.

'Oh, but I don't want protection,' Fanny had laughed, and when Julia Craye, fixing on her that extraordinary look, had said she was not so sure of that, Fanny positively blushed under the admiration in her eyes.

It was the only use of men, she had said. Was it for that reason then, Fanny wondered with her eyes on the floor, that she had never married? After all, she had not lived all her life in Salisbury. 'Much the nicest part of London,' she had said once, '(but I'm speaking of fifteen or twenty years ago) is Kensington.' One was in the Gardens in ten minutes—it was like the heart of the country. One could dine out in one's slippers without catching cold. 'Kensington was like a village then, you know,' she said.

Here she broke off, to denounce, acridly, the draughts in the Tubes. 'It was the use of men,' she had said, with a queer, wry acerbity. Did that throw any light on the problem why she had not married? One could imagine every sort of scene in her youth, when with her good, blue eyes, her straight, firm nose, her piano playing, her rose flowering with chaste passion in the bosom of her muslin dress, she had attracted first the young men to whom such things, and the china tea-cups and the silver candlesticks, and the inlaid tables (for the Crayes had such nice things) were wonderful; young men not sufficiently distinguished; young men of the cathedral town with ambitions. She had attracted them first, and then her brother's friends from Oxford or

Cambridge. They would come down in the summer, row her up the river, continue the argument about Browning* by letter, and arrange perhaps on the rare occasions when she stayed in London to show her—Kensington Gardens?

'Much the nicest part of London—Kensington. I'm speaking of fifteen or twenty years ago,' she had said once. One was in the gardens in ten minutes—in the heart of the country. One could make that yield what one liked, Fanny Wilmot thought, single out for instance, Mr Sherman, the painter, and old friend of hers; make him call for her by appointment one sunny day in June; take her to have tea under the trees. (They had met, too, at those parties to which one tripped in slippers without fear of catching cold.) The aunt or other elderly relative was to wait there while they looked at the Serpentine.* They looked at the Serpentine. He may have rowed her across. They compared it with the Avon.* She would have considered the comparison very seriously, for views of rivers were important to her. She sat hunched a little, a little angular, though she was graceful then, steering. At the critical moment, for he had determined that he must speak now—it was his only chance of getting her alone—he was speaking with his head turned at an absurd angle, in his great nervousness, over his shoulder—at that very moment she interrupted fiercely. He would have them into the Bridge,* she cried. It was a moment of horror, of disillusionment, of revelation for both of them. 'I can't have it, I can't possess it,' she thought. He could not see why she had come then. With a great splash of his oar he pulled the boat round. Merely to snub him? He rowed her back and said good-by to her.

The setting of that scene could be varied as one chose, Fanny Wilmot reflected. (Where had that pin fallen?) It might be Ravenna*—or Edinburgh, where she had kept house for her brother. The scene could be changed and the young man and the exact manner of it all; but one thing was constant—her refusal and her frown and her anger with herself afterward and her argument and her relief—yes, certainly her immense relief. The very next day perhaps she would get up at six, put on her cloak, and walk all the way from Kensington to the river. She was so thankful that she had not sacrificed her right to go and look at things when they are at their best—before people are up, that is to say. She could have her breakfast in bed if she liked. She had not sacrificed her independence.

Yes, Fanny Wilmot smiled, Julia had not endangered her habits. They remained safe, and her habits would have suffered if she had married. 'They're ogres,' she had said one evening, half laughing, when another pupil, a girl lately married, suddenly bethinking her that she would miss her husband, had rushed off in haste.

'They're ogres,' she had said, laughing grimly. An ogre would have interfered perhaps with breakfast in bed, with walks at dawn down to the river. What would have happened (but one could hardly conceive this) had she had children? She took astonishing precautions against chills, fatigue, rich food, the wrong food, draughts, heated rooms, journeys in the Tube, for she could never determine which of these it was exactly that brought on those terrible headaches that gave her life the semblance of a battlefield. She was always engaged in outwitting the enemy, until it seemed as if the pursuit had its interest; could she have beaten the enemy finally she would have found life a little dull. As it was, the tug of war was perpetual—on the one side, the nightingale or the view which she loved with passion—yes, for views and birds she felt nothing less than passion; on the other, the damp path or the horrid, long drag up a steep hill which would certainly make her good for nothing next day and bring on one of her headaches. When, therefore, from time to time, she managed her forces adroitly and brought off a visit to Hampton Court* the week the crocuses (those glossy, bright flowers were her favourites) were at their best, it was a victory. It was something that lasted, something that mattered forever. She strung the afternoon on the necklace of memorable days which was not too long for her to be able to recall this one or that one; this view, that city; to finger it, to feel it, to savour, sighing, the quality that made it unique.

'It was so beautiful last Friday,' she said, 'that I determined I must go there.' So she had gone off to Waterloo* on her great undertaking—to visit Hampton Court—alone. Naturally, but perhaps foolishly, one pitied her for the thing she never asked pity for (indeed she was reticent habitually, speaking of her health only as a warrior might speak of his foe)—one pitied her for always doing everything alone. Her brother was dead. Her sister was asthmatic. She found the climate of Edinburgh good for her. It was too bleak for Julia. Perhaps too she found the associations painful, for her brother, the famous archæologist, had died there; and she had loved her brother. She lived in a little house off the Brompton Road* entirely alone.

Fanny Wilmot saw the pin on the carpet; she picked it up. She looked at Miss Craye; was Miss Craye so lonely? No, Miss Craye was steadily, blissfully, if only for a moment, a happy woman. Fanny had surprised her in a moment of ecstasy. She sat there, half turned away from the piano, with her hands clasped in her lap holding the carnation upright, while behind her was the sharp square of the window, uncurtained, purple in the evening, intensely purple after the brilliant electric lights which burnt unshaded in the bare music room. Julia Craye sitting hunched and compact holding her flower seemed to emerge out of the London night, seemed to fling it like a cloak behind her. It seemed in its bareness and intensity the effluence of her spirit, something she had made which surrounded her, which was her. Fanny stared.

All seemed transparent for a moment to the gaze of Fanny Wilmot, as if looking through Miss Craye, she saw the very fountain of her being spurt up in pure, silver drops. She saw back and back into the past behind her. She saw the green Roman vases stood in their case; heard the choristers playing cricket; saw Julia quietly descend the curving steps on to the lawn; saw her pour out tea beneath the cedar tree; softly enclose the old man's hand in hers; saw her going round and about the corridors of that ancient Cathedral dwelling place with towels in her hand to mark them; lamenting as she went the pettiness of daily life; and slowly aging, and putting away clothes when summer came, because at her age they were too bright to wear; and tending her father's sickness; and cleaving her way ever more definitely as her will stiffened toward her solitary goal; travelling frugally; counting the cost and measuring out of her tight shut purse the sum needed for this journey, or for that old mirror; obstinately adhering whatever people might say in choosing her pleasures for herself. She saw Julia—

She saw Julia open her arms; saw her blaze; saw her kindle. Out of the night she burnt like a dead white star. Julia kissed her. Julia possessed her.

'Slater's pins have no points,' Miss Craye said, laughing queerly and relaxing her arms, as Fanny Wilmot pinned the flower to her breast with trembling fingers.

THE LADY IN THE LOOKING-GLASS:
A REFLECTION

PEOPLE should not leave looking-glasses hanging in their rooms any more than they should leave open cheque books or letters confessing some hideous crime. One could not help looking, that summer afternoon, in the long glass that hung outside in the hall. Chance had so arranged it. From the depths of the sofa in the drawing-room one could see reflected in the Italian glass not only the marble-topped table opposite, but a stretch of the garden beyond. One could see a long grass path leading between banks of tall flowers until, slicing off an angle, the gold rim cut it off.

The house was empty, and one felt, since one was the only person in the drawing-room, like one of those naturalists who, covered with grass and leaves, lie watching the shyest animals—badgers, otters, kingfishers—moving about freely, themselves unseen. The room that afternoon was full of such shy creatures, lights and shadows, curtains blowing, petals falling—things that never happen, so it seems, if someone is looking. The quiet old country room with its rugs and stone chimney pieces, its sunken book-cases and red and gold lacquer cabinets, was full of such nocturnal creatures. They came pirouetting across the floor, stepping delicately with high-lifted feet and spread tails and pecking allusive beaks as if they had been cranes or flocks of elegant flamingoes whose pink was faded, or peacocks whose trains were veined with silver. And there were obscure flushes and darkenings too, as if a cuttlefish had suddenly suffused the air with purple; and the room had its passions and rages and envies and sorrows coming over it and clouding it, like a human being. Nothing stayed the same for two seconds together.

But, outside, the looking-glass reflected the hall table, the sunflowers, the garden path so accurately and so fixedly that they seemed held there in their reality unescapably. It was a strange contrast—all changing here, all stillness there. One could not help looking from one to the other. Meanwhile, since all the doors and windows were open in the heat, there was a perpetual sighing and ceasing sound, the voice of the transient and the perishing, it seemed, coming and going like human breath, while in the looking-glass things had ceased to breathe and lay still in the trance of immortality.

Half an hour ago the mistress of the house, Isabella Tyson, had gone down the grass path in her thin summer dress, carrying a basket, and had vanished, sliced off by the gilt rim of the looking-glass. She had gone presumably into the lower garden to pick flowers; or as it seemed more natural to suppose, to pick something light and fantastic and leafy and trailing, traveller's joy, or one of those elegant sprays of convolvulus that twine round ugly walls and burst here and there into white and violet blossoms. She suggested the fantastic and the tremulous convolvulus rather than the upright aster, the starched zinnia, or her own burning roses alight like lamps on the straight posts of their rose trees. The comparison showed how very little, after all these years, one knew about her; for it is impossible that any woman of flesh and blood of fifty-five or sixty should be really a wreath or a tendril. Such comparisons are worse than idle and superficial—they are cruel even, for they come like the convolvulus itself trembling between one's eyes and the truth. There must be truth; there must be a wall. Yet it was strange that after knowing her all these years one could not say what the truth about Isabella was; one still made up phrases like this about convolvulus and traveller's joy. As for facts, it was a fact that she was a spinster; that she was rich; that she had bought this house and collected with her own hands—often in the most obscure corners of the world and at great risk from poisonous stings and Oriental diseases—the rugs, the chairs, the cabinets which now lived their nocturnal life before one's eyes. Sometimes it seemed as if they knew more about her than we, who sat on them, wrote at them, and trod on them so carefully, were allowed to know. In each of these cabinets were many little drawers, and each almost certainly held letters, tied with bows of ribbon, sprinkled with sticks of lavender or rose leaves. For it was another fact—if facts were what one wanted—that Isabella had known many people, had had many friends; and thus if one had the audacity to open a drawer and read her letters, one would find the traces of many agitations, of appointments to meet, of upbraidings for not having met, long letters of intimacy and affection, violent letters of jealousy and reproach, terrible final words of parting—for all those interviews and assignations had led to nothing—that is, she had never married, and yet, judging from the mask-like indifference of her face, she had gone through twenty times more of passion and experience than those whose loves are trumpeted forth for all the world to hear. Under the stress of thinking about Isabella, her room became more shadowy and symbolic; the corners seemed darker, the legs of chairs and tables more spindly and hieroglyphic.

Suddenly these reflections were ended violently and yet without a sound. A large black form loomed into the looking-glass; blotted out everything, strewed the table with a packet of marble tablets veined with pink and grey, and was gone. But the picture was entirely altered. For the moment it was unrecognizable and irrational and entirely out of focus. One could not relate these tablets to any human purpose. And then by degrees some logical process set to work on them and began ordering and arranging them and bringing them into the fold of common experience. One realized at last that they were merely letters. The man had brought the post.

There they lay on the marble-topped table, all dripping with light and colour at first and crude and unabsorbed. And then it was strange to see how they were drawn in and arranged and composed and made part of the picture and granted that stillness and immortality which the looking-glass conferred. They lay there invested with a new reality and significance and with a greater heaviness, too, as if it would have needed a chisel to dislodge them from the table. And, whether it was fancy or not, they seemed to have become not merely a handful of casual letters but to be tablets graven with eternal truth—if one could read them, one would know everything there was to be known about Isabella, yes, and about life, too. The pages inside those marble-looking envelopes must be cut deep and scored thick with meaning. Isabella would come in, and take them, one by one, very slowly, and open them, and read them carefully word by word, and then with a profound sigh of comprehension, as if she had seen to the bottom of everything, she would tear the envelopes to little bits and tie the letters together and lock the cabinet drawer in her determination to conceal what she did not wish to be known.

The thought served as a challenge. Isabella did not wish to be known—but she should no longer escape. It was absurd, it was monstrous. If she concealed so much and knew so much one must prize her open with the first tool that came to hand—the imagination. One must fix one's mind upon her at that very moment. One must fasten her down there. One must refuse to be put off any longer with sayings and doings such as the moment brought forth—with dinners and visits and polite conversations. One must put oneself in her shoes. If one took the phrase literally, it was easy to see the shoes in which she stood, down in the lower garden, at this moment. They were very narrow and long and fashionable—they were made of the softest and most flexible leather. Like everything she wore, they were exquisite. And she would be standing under the high hedge in the lower part of the garden, raising the scissors that were tied to her waist to cut some dead flower, some overgrown branch. The sun would beat down on her face, into her eyes; but no, at the critical moment a veil of cloud covered the sun, making the expression of her eyes doubtful—was it mocking or tender, brilliant or dull? One could only see the indeterminate outline of her rather faded, fine face looking at the sky. She was thinking, perhaps, that she must order a new net for the strawberries; that she must send flowers to Johnson's widow; that it was time she drove over to see the Hippesleys in their new house. Those were the things she talked about at dinner certainly. But one was tired of the things that she talked about at dinner. It was her profounder state of being that one wanted to catch and turn to words, the state that is to the mind what breathing is to the body, what one calls happiness or unhappiness. At the mention of those words it became obvious, surely, that she must be happy. She was rich; she was distinguished; she had many friends; she travelled—she bought rugs in Turkey and blue pots in Persia. Avenues of pleasure radiated this way and that from where she stood with her scissors raised to cut the trembling branches while the lacy clouds veiled her face.

Here with a quick movement of her scissors she snipped the spray of traveller's joy and it fell to the ground. As it fell, surely some light came in too, surely one could penetrate a little farther into her being. Her mind then was filled with tenderness and regret . . . To cut an overgrown branch saddened her because it had once lived, and life was dear to her. Yes, and at the same time the fall of the branch would suggest to her how she must die herself and all the futility and evanescence of things. And then again quickly catching this thought up, with her instant good sense, she thought life had treated her well; even if fall she must, it was to lie on the earth and moulder sweetly into the roots of violets. So she stood thinking. Without making any thought precise—for she was one of those reticent people whose minds hold their thoughts enmeshed in clouds of silence—she was filled with thoughts. Her mind was like her room, in which lights advanced and retreated, came pirouetting and stepping delicately, spread their tails, pecked their way; and then her whole being was suffused, like the room again, with a cloud of some profound know-ledge, some unspoken regret, and then she was full of locked drawers, stuffed with letters, like her cabinets. To talk of 'prizing her open' as if she were an oyster, to use any but the finest and subtlest and most pliable tools upon her was impious and absurd. One must imagine—here was she in the looking-glass. It made one start.

She was so far off at first that one could not see her clearly. She came lingering and pausing, here straightening a rose, there lifting a pink to smell it, but she never stopped; and all the time she became larger and larger in the looking-glass, more and more completely the person into whose mind one had been trying to penetrate. One veri-fied her by degrees—fitted the qualities one had discovered into this visible body. There were her grey-green dress, and her long shoes, her basket, and something sparkling at her throat. She came so gradually that she did not seem to derange the pattern in the glass, but only to bring in some new element which gently moved and altered the other objects as if asking them, courteously, to make room for her. And the letters and the table and the grass walk and the sunflowers which had been waiting in the looking-glass separated and opened out so that she might be received among them. At last there she was, in the hall. She stopped dead. She stood by the table. She stood perfectly still. At once the looking-glass began to pour over her a light that seemed to fix her; that seemed like some acid to bite off the unessential and superficial and to leave only the truth. It was an enthralling spectacle. Everything dropped from her—clouds, dress, basket, diamond—all that one had called the creeper and convolvulus. Here was the hard wall beneath. Here was the woman herself. She stood naked in that pitiless light. And there was nothing. Isabella was perfectly empty. She had no thoughts. She had no friends. She cared for nobody. As for her letters, they were all bills. Look, as she stood there, old and angular, veined and lined, with her high nose and her wrinkled neck, she did not even trouble to open them.

People should not leave looking-glasses hanging in their rooms.

APPENDIX
TEXTUAL VARIANTS

THREE of the stories reprinted here from *Monday or Tuesday* were first published elsewhere; indeed, 'The Mark on the Wall' appeared in two different editions before the publication of *Monday or Tuesday*, in 1917 and in 1919, and an extract was also published as a single-sheet 'broadside'. In preparing the stories for publication in *Monday or Tuesday*, Woolf made some amendments to the first published versions. These amendments are summarized below; substantial or highly significant changes are recorded in full, with the text from this edition given in italics, followed by the version in the first edition.

It is also worth noting how Woolf chose to arrange the stories in *Monday or Tuesday*. 'An Unwritten Novel' appeared in the middle of the collection, 'Kew Gardens' was the penultimate piece, and 'The Mark on the Wall'—Woolf's first published short fiction—concluded the collection.

The Mark on the Wall

'The Mark on the Wall' was first published in *Two Stories*, the first ever publication of the Woolfs' Hogarth Press (see Introduction, pp. xii, xv). The story was reprinted in 1919, as a stand-alone publication *The Mark on the Wall*, with just a couple of corrections to printing errors. However, Woolf made a number of revisions to the text for publication in *Monday or Tuesday* (1921) including the introduction of several more instances of ellipses (usually four dots, which we have standardized to three) in the place of full stops. A number of commas are added, many more than are removed. A couple of dashes are also added; and 'ise/isation' endings become 'ize/ization'. There are a few other minor changes to punctuation, including to hyphenation, and a couple of corrections to obvious grammatical errors. More substantial variants are recorded below, including the removal of a lengthy passage describing a housekeeper, and the small, but significant, change to the final line.

3.27 *happened next. They wanted*] happened next. She wore a flannel dog collar round her throat, and he drew posters for an oatmeal company, and they wanted

4.38 *believe. / The tree*] believe. But I know a house-keeper, a woman with the profile of a police-man, those little round buttons marked even upon the edge of her shadow, a woman with a broom in her hand, a thumb on picture frames, an eye under beds and she talks always of art. She is coming nearer and nearer; and now, pointing to certain spots of yellow rust on the fender, she becomes so menacing that to oust her, I shall have to end her by taking action: I shall have to get up and see for myself what that mark—

But no. I refuse to be beaten. I will not move. I will not recognise her. See, she fades already. I am very nearly rid of her and her insinuations, which I can hear quite distinctly. Yet she has about her the pathos of all people who wish to compromise. And why should I resent the fact that she has a few books in her house, a picture or two? But what I really resent is that she resents me—life being an affair of attack and defence after all. Another time I will have it out with her, not now. She must go now. The tree

5.35 *the vagueness, the gleam of glassiness, in our eyes.*] the expression in our vague and almost glassy eyes.

7.13 *opposed, indites*] opposed, casts all his arrowheads into one scale, and being still further opposed, indites

9.19 *The Downs? Whitaker's Almanack? The fields of asphodel?*] The Downs, Whitaker's Almanack, the fields of asphodel?

9.28 *It was a snail.*] For it was a snail.

Kew Gardens

There are very few differences between the first published version of 'Kew Gardens' (May 1919) and the version included in *Monday or Tuesday*: all are minor and most are amendments to punctuation.

An Unwritten Novel

A number of revisions were made to 'An Unwritten Novel' (first published July 1920) for the *Monday or Tuesday* version, mainly amendments to punctuation (particularly removal of commas). Key amendments, including changes to punctuation that make a significant difference to the meaning of the passage in question, are listed below.

17.21 *were as*] were damp as

19.2 *hills*] bills

19.28 *ribbons.*] ribbons all along the counters.

20.9 *But elderly women are the worst.*] "But elderly women are the worst."

20.17 *helped. And*] helped. You take the sponge, the pumice-stone, you scrape and scrub, you squirm and sluice; it can't be done—let me try;

I can't reach it either—the spot between the shoulders—cold water only—why should she grudge that? And

22.29 *opposite and*] opposite (I can't bear to watch her!) and

23.17 *'Dear, dear!'*] Dear, dear!

23.29 *the sepulchral*] the sinister and the sepulchral

25.27 *street? Where*] street, where

EXPLANATORY NOTES

THE MARK ON THE WALL

3 *the miniature of a lady with white powdered curls, powder-dusted cheeks, and lips like red carnations*: a miniature portrait of this appearance was likely to date from the late eighteenth century.

4 *the Queen Anne coal-scuttle*: almost certainly of the Queen Anne revival, a period in the decorative arts of the late nineteenth century, rather than dating from the period of Queen Anne's reign (1702–14).

bagatelle board: bagatelle is an indoor table game in which participants have to use wooden cues to hit balls into holes without knocking over wooden pins. Boards were quite large, varying in length between 6 and 10 feet (1.8 to 3 metres).

hand organ: a pipe organ played by manually turning a crank to operate a bellows.

the Tube: the London Underground.

asphodel meadows: in Greek myth, the realm of the dead, where the everlasting flowers of the asphodel grow. As described in Homer's epic *Odyssey*, it is an eerie and shadowy realm, where ordinary souls dwelt, while heroes were permitted access to the paradise of Elysium; some later poets however depicted it more positively.

buried Troy three times over: Troy was a fortress city located in what is now Turkey, near the Dardanelles where the Aegean Sea flows through a narrow inlet into the Sea of Marmara. The Trojan War, fought between the Greeks and the Trojans, is the most significant subject of classical literature, forming the basis of Homer's *Iliad*; the story of the Greek leaders' return home after their victory over the city is told in his *Odyssey*. Troy was excavated many times in the late nineteenth century, with these digs revealing at the time nine levels of archaeological remains.

5 *Kingsway*: a thoroughfare in central London opened in 1905 as part of a redevelopment of this part of the capital; it runs north–south between Holborn and Aldwych.

Charles the First: Charles I (1600–49) was king of England, Scotland, and Northern Ireland from 1625 until his execution in 1649.

Tall flowers with purple tassels to them perhaps: very likely aquilegias, also known as columbines, which self-seed easily and thus frequently grow wild.

6 *Whitaker's Table of Precedency*: Whitaker's *Almanack*, published annually since 1868, contains a section entitled 'Precedence', which lists the complete social hierarchy of the United Kingdom from the sovereign down, including religious (as Woolf records), parliamentary, military,

legal, and inherited aristocratic positions, and positions in the royal household.

6 *Landseer prints*: Sir Edwin Henry Landseer (1802–73) was an English artist, celebrated for his portraits of animals which were widely available as reproductions. He also made the sculptures of four lions which surround Trafalgar Square in central London.

a small tumulus like those barrows on the South Downs . . . either tombs or camps: the South Downs are a range of chalk hills in south-east England, running from Hampshire to West Sussex and ending at Beachy Head in East Sussex. The Woolfs lived for many years in the village of Rodmell, located at the foot of the South Downs near Lewes, East Sussex. Tumuli and barrows strictly speaking refer to man-made mounds of earth used to mark graves in prehistoric times, although here the narrator refers to features whose purpose is apparently not agreed upon. In *The Voyage Out* (1915) Woolf alludes to the scholarly dispute as to the function of these features; one of her characters does not ' "believe that the circular mounds or barrows which we find on the top of our English downs were camps. The antiquaries call everything a camp." '

9 *Curse this war!*: 'The Mark on the Wall' was published in 1917, three years into the First World War.

KEW GARDENS

10 *hundred stalks . . . clubbed at the end*: although previous editors have identified these as gladioli (Bradshaw, in his edition of Virginia Woolf, *The Mark on the Wall and Other Stories*, Oxford World's Classics (Oxford: Oxford University Press, 2001), 101), the flower which most closely fits this description is in fact the tulip—particularly its clubbed stigma. The fact that there are no blue tulips—though there are purple ones— suggests that it is play with (primary) colour, rather than absolute fidelity to reality, which is Woolf's primary concern here. In fact, during the time that Woolf was composing 'Kew Gardens', many of its oval flower beds were dug up and planted with onions and potatoes as part of the war effort (see Eliza Kay Sparks, '(No) "Loopholes of Retreat": The Cultural Context of Parks and Gardens in Woolf's Life and Work', in Merry M. Pawlowski and Eileen Barrett (eds), *Woolf: Across the Generations; Selected Papers from the Twelfth International Conference on Virginia Woolf* (Clemson, SC: Clemson University Digital Press, 2003).

the men and women who walk in Kew Gardens in July: a botanic garden was first founded at Kew, now part of the London Borough of Richmond upon Thames in south-west London, in 1759; the Royal Botanic Gardens were opened to the public in 1840 and by the time of the composition of 'Kew Gardens' had become an extremely popular visitor destination.

Lily: a central character in one of Woolf's most celebrated novels, *To the Lighthouse* (1927), is an artist called Lily Briscoe.

11 *the mother of all my kisses all my life*: this passage bears similarities with one in Woolf's 1925 novel *Mrs Dalloway*, in which the protagonist Clarissa remembers 'the most exquisite moment of her whole life passing a stone urn with flowers in it. Sally stopped; picked a flower; kissed her on the lips.' See Virginia Woolf, *Mrs Dalloway*, ed. David Bradshaw, Oxford World's Classics (Oxford: OUP, 2000), 30.

12 *Thessaly*: a north-eastern region of modern Greece, known for its fertile soils, and enclosed by mountains. The Thessalians were for a period the dominant power in central Greece. The region was also famed for the supposed magical powers of some of its women, particularly their capacity to draw down the moon.

13 *the forests of Uruguay . . . women drowned at sea*: Woolf's first novel, *The Voyage Out* (1915), had, perhaps surprisingly, been set in South America (where Woolf had never been), and features a young female protagonist entering into womanhood.

14 *'They make you pay sixpence on Friday'*: an entrance fee for the Royal Botanic Gardens was introduced in 1916. The fee was one penny except on Sundays (which were free), and Tuesdays and Fridays when sixpence was charged for a full day; these were designated 'student' days for study, sketching, and photography. On Friday, 23 November 1917, Woolf 'settled that if it was the 6d day at Kew I wouldn't hesitate but decide not to go in. It was the 6d day; I turned without pausing and had therefore to walk back. Certainly this decision brings a feeling of peace, though I rather think I was wrong' (*The Diary of Virginia Woolf*, ed. Anne Olivier Bell and Andrew McNeillie (5 vols; London: Hogarth Press, 1977–84), i. 81).

what sort of tea they gave you at Kew: there had been a refreshment pavilion at Kew, in response to popular demand, since 1888. It was rebuilt after being burned down as a political protest by suffragettes, campaigning for votes for women, in 1913.

15 *Chinese pagoda*: the Great Pagoda was one of several Chinese buildings designed for Kew in the eighteenth century. It was completed in 1762 as a gift for Princess Augusta, the founder of the gardens, and is 164 feet (50 metres) high.

palm house: the Palm House at Kew was completed in 1844. The first structure of its kind to use wrought-iron supports, its hand-blown glass panels were originally green in colour to help control the temperature inside the building. The central nave is 62 feet (19 metres) high.

Chinese boxes: a set of boxes of graduated size each designed to fit inside the next.

AN UNWRITTEN NOVEL

16 *map of the line framed opposite*: railway carriages of the period displayed a map of the line above the seats for passengers' information. The line in question is that from London Victoria to Eastbourne, a coastal resort in

East Sussex, which Woolf took regularly as she journeyed between her London and Sussex homes. The line passed through Three Bridges and Lewes (both mentioned later in this story). Woolf would have alighted at Lewes to get to Asham (or Asheham) House, near Beddingham, which she and her sister jointly rented for holidays and weekends from October 1912; and later Monk's House, Rodmell, which she and her husband Leonard bought in July 1919.

16 *Peace between Germany and the Allied Powers . . . it's all in the Times!*: The *Times* was, and remains, the best known British daily newspaper, established in 1785. The First World War had been brought to an end by Armistice in November 1918, followed by the signing of the Treaty of Versailles (at the palace of the same name just outside Paris), on 28 June 1919; the treaty was ratified six months later on 10 January 1920. Present at both the signing and the ratification of the treaty was Francesco Saverio Nitti (1868–1953), prime minister of Italy from June 1919 until June 1920 when he resigned after a turbulent period in office. Doncaster is a large railway town in the north of England. The Court Circular is the official record of past engagements of the royal family, printed in *The Times*. The 'Sandhills murder' refers to the murder of Kathleen Elsie Breaks on the sand dunes in St Annes, Lancashire, on Christmas Eve, 1919; *The Times* first reported the case with the headline 'Seaside Murder Charge: Woman's Body Found Among Sandhills' on 27 December 1919. But as David Bradshaw has pointed out, these news items 'are not "all in *The Times*" for Sunday, 11 January 1920 (the day in question if "Peace . . . was *yesterday* officially ushered in at Paris," as *The Times* is said to report) as the newspaper was not (and is not) published on a Sunday. Nor do these items of news appear together in another issue of *The Times* from around this date' (David Bradshaw, in Woolf, *The Mark on the Wall*, 102).

18 *Hilda*: the name 'Hilda' evokes the title, and protagonist, of Arnold Bennett's 1911 novel *Hilda Lessways*, a work which Woolf would go on to lambast by name in her 1923 essay 'Mr Bennett and Mrs Brown'. See also note to p. 51.

Minnie: the first wife of Woolf's father Leslie Stephen, Harriet Marian Stephen (née Ritchie) (1840–75), was known as Minny or Minnie.

19 *President Kruger . . . Prince Albert*: Stephanus Johannes Paulus Kruger (1825–1904) led the Boer rebellion against Britain in 1880, and went on to become president of the South African Republic from 1883 to 1902. Stout, bewhiskered, and forthright, he would have appeared in significant contrast to Prince Albert (1819–61), prince consort of Queen Victoria from 1840, who, while like Kruger a deeply religious man, was tall, attractive, and cultured.

Croydon: by the early twentieth century, this Surrey market town had expanded to become a popular residential area, particularly among commuters to London owing to its good railway link to the City.

21 *Down the slopes of the Andes . . . gold and silver*: the Andes range of mountains stretch the length of the western side of South America, and are
partly made of marble. The narrator refigures the tumbling eggshells as
the successful ambush of a Spanish treasure train by Sir Francis Drake
(*c*.1540–96) and his men in 1573, on the outskirts of Nombre de Dios,
a port city on the northern coast of the Isthmus of Panama. The Andes do
not in fact reach as far north as Nombre de Dios, their northernmost end
being in Colombia.

22 *glacis*: a gentle slope, particularly by way of fortification.

travels in—shall we say buttons?: works as a travelling salesman, selling
buttons.

Truth: a weekly newspaper published between 1877 and 1957, particularly
known for its investigative journalism.

23 *St Paul's*: St Paul's Cathedral, designed by Sir Christopher Wren (1632–
1723), completed in 1710, and one of the City of London's great land-
marks with its unmistakable domed roof.

24 *merrythought*: archaic term for the wishbone of a bird, thought to bring
good luck.

SOLID OBJECTS

26 *pilchard boat*: this makes the setting most likely Cornwall, home of the
pilchard fishing industry through the eighteenth and nineteenth centuries.
As a child, Woolf took her holidays in St Ives, Cornwall, and vividly
described the pilchards 'coming in' in an early journal, as well as recalling
such scenes in her later memoirs (*A Passionate Apprentice: The Early
Journals 1897–1909*, ed. Mitchell A. Leaska (London: Hogarth Press,
1990), 292–3; *Moments of Being*, ed, Jeanne Shulkind (1976; Orlando, FL:
Harcourt Brace & Co., 1985), 130).

'Politics be damned!': a widely used idiom; the German politician and
theologian Christoph Blumhart (1842–1919) is quoted as having said
(translated from the German) 'I am proud to stand before you as a man;
and if politics cannot tolerate a human being, then let politics be damned.'

28 *Temple*: referring collectively to the Inner and Middle Temple Inns of
Court, situated between the Strand and the river Thames in central
London. All barristers practising in England and Wales must belong to
one of the four ancient Inns of Court (the other two being Gray's Inn and
Lincoln's Inn).

30 *Barnes Common*: around 120 acres (485,623 square metres) of grass and
woodland in Barnes, then in Surrey, now part of the London Borough of
Richmond upon Thames in south-west London.

A HAUNTED HOUSE

32 *Downs*: see note to p. 6.

MONDAY OR TUESDAY

34 *a cry . . . midday*: this is a slightly revised version of a passage found in a story named 'Sympathy', probably written in the spring of 1919. 'Sympathy' exists in a typescript, revised by Woolf, but was not published in her lifetime. It first appeared in *The Complete Shorter Fiction of Virginia Woolf*, ed. Susan Dick (1985; London: Hogarth Press, rev. edn 1989), 108–11.

Flaunted, leaf-light . . . sunk, assembled: the syncopated rhythms and alliterative vocabulary of this passage are strikingly similar to those found in the poetry of Gerard Manley Hopkins (1844–89). Almost unpublished in his own lifetime, his collected *Poems* appeared in 1918. On 23 July 1919, Woolf wrote to her friend Janet Case: 'Have you read the poems of a man, who is dead, called Gerard Hopkins? I like them better than any poetry for ever so long; partly because they're so difficult, but also because instead of writing mere rhythms and sense as most poets do, he makes a very strange jumble; so that what is apparently pure nonsense is at the same time very beautiful, and not nonsense at all' (*The Letters of Virginia Woolf*, ed. Nigel Nicolson and Joanne Trautmann (6 vols; London: Hogarth Press, 1975–80), ii. 379). On 5 January 1920, she sent Case the poems, quoting 'Heaven-Haven' and adding 'Yes, I should like to have written that myself' (*Letters*, ii. 415).

BLUE AND GREEN

36 *lustre*: an ornament popular in the nineteenth century, featuring cut-glass pendants, which may be placed on a mantelpiece; may also refer to a glass chandelier or candelabrum. Woolf was apparently fond of such ornaments; she enquired of her sister (the artist Vanessa Bell) as to whether, as part of the redecoration of Monk's House in June 1926, she might be 'allowed some rather garish but vibrating and radiating green and red lustres on the mantelpiece? Showers of glass, shaped like long fingers in a bunch—you know my taste that way' (*Letters*, iii. 273).

THE STRING QUARTET

38 *landaus with bays*: four-wheeled carriages with two folding hoods, here pulled by bay (reddish-brown) horses; a luxury form of urban transport.

Regent Street is up, and the Treaty signed: Regent Street was London's first purpose-built shopping street, featuring numerous high-end department stores. Sandra Kemp suggests that 'Regent Street is up' means that the shops are closed for repairs (in *Virginia Woolf: Selected Short Stories*, ed. Susan Kemp (London: Penguin, 1993), 113). For 'the Treaty', see note to p. 16.

influenza: the worldwide influenza (or 'Spanish flu') pandemic of 1918–19 killed more people than had died in the First World War: more than 228,000 in the United Kingdom.

The King: George V (1865–1936; r. 1910–36).

Malmesbury: a small market town in Wiltshire, south-west England.

39 *old, jolly fishwives, squatted under arches, obscene old women*: this passage
   recalls Rachel Vinrace's fever-induced vision of 'little deformed women
   sitting in archways playing cards' in *The Voyage Out* (1915; Oxford:
   Oxford University Press, 2001), 386.

40 *Sorrow, sorrow. Joy, joy. Woven together*: this passage may echo Blake's
   'Auguries of Innocence', in particular the lines 'Joy and woe are woven
   fine, | A clothing for the soul divine.' Blake's poem is structured around
   contrasting dualisms, also a feature of this part of Woolf's story.

41 *seneschals*: another word for stewards, heads of the domestic arrangements
   of a sovereign or noble.

A SOCIETY

42 *London Library*: a private members' library in central London, founded in
   1841. Woolf's father, Sir Leslie Stephen (1832–1904) was the library's
   president from 1892 until his death; Woolf herself joined only four days
   after he died.

   'From a Window' . . . *of that kind*: the work alluded to appears to be *From
   a College Window* (1906), a collection of essays by the academic and prolific
   writer A. C. (Arthur Christopher) Benson. He was Master of Magdalene
   College, University of Cambridge, from 1915 until his death in 1925.

43 *Lives of the Lord Chancellors*: the full title of this seven-volume work by
   John Lord Campbell is *The Lives of the Lord Chancellors and Keepers of the
   Great Seal of England from the Earliest Times till the Reign of King George
   IV* (1845–7). See 'The Mark on the Wall', p. 91, for Woolf's ironic discus-
   sion of Lord (High) Chancellors.

   Clorinda: the name of a Saracen warrior woman in the epic poem
   Gerusalemme liberata (*Jerusalem Delivered*) (1581) by the Italian poet
   Torquato Tasso (1544–95). In depicting Clorinda as a white daughter of
   black parentage, Tasso appears to have drawn on the character Chariclea
   from the ancient Greek *Ethiopian Story of Theagenes and Chariclea* by the
   fourth-century writer Heliodorus of Emesa.

   to produce good people and good books: these principles are central to the
   thought of G. E. Moore, whose *Principia Ethica* (1903) was revered as the
   guiding philosophical text for many of Woolf's closest Bloomsbury peers
   who encountered his work while students at Cambridge. He insisted on
   the intrinsic value of beauty, love, truth, and—in particular—goodness,
   which he argued was the most fundamental, and irreducible, ethical
   concept.

44 *Royal Academy and the Tate*: for the Royal Academy, see note to p. 45. The
   Tate Gallery, dedicated to British art, was established at Millbank in London
   in 1897, named after its founding donor the industrialist Henry Tate.

44 *Ethiopian Prince . . . taps upon the behind*: a clear reference to the so-called
Dreadnought Hoax of February 1910, in which Woolf, her brother Adrian,
and three friends including the painter Duncan Grant, disguised themselves as the Emperor of Abyssinia and his entourage, and were given an
official reception on board the HMS *Dreadnought*, at the time the Navy's
most technologically advanced warship. When the hoax was revealed,
Grant was given the token punishment from a naval officer of two taps on
the bottom with a cane (see Hermione Lee, *Virginia Woolf* (London:
Chatto & Windus, 1996), 282–7).

Trafalgar: the naval battle of Trafalgar in 1805 during the Napoleonic
Wars. It was a decisive victory for the British forces, led by Lord Nelson,
over the French, and confirmed Britain's naval supremacy.

45 *Law Courts*: the informal name for the Royal Courts of Justice, housing
the highest courts in England and Wales, and located on the Strand in
central London (see note to p. 67).

Helen: another name in this story with classical associations. In Greek
myth, Helen was the daughter of Zeus, famed for her beauty. Having
married King Menelaus of Sparta, she was abducted by, or eloped with
(interpretations differ), Prince Paris of Troy, son of King Priam, sparking
off the Trojan War (see note to p. 4 and also notes to names on pp. 43, 45,
and 47).

Royal Academy: referring to the home, since 1867, of the Royal Academy
of Arts at Burlington House, central London.

'O for the touch . . . the way to glory—': this list of more or less accurate
quotations from a range of literary sources expresses that, according to
Helen's report, the paintings exhibited at the Royal Academy are frequently inspired by literary sources, along broadly sentimental, patriotic,
militaristic, or nostalgic lines. The sources are: 'But O for the touch of
a vanish'd hand, | And the sound of a voice that is still!', from 'Break,
Break, Break' (1842) by Alfred Lord Tennyson (1809–92); 'Home is the
sailor, home from the sea, | And the hunter home from the hill', from
Underwoods (1887) (XXI, 'Requiem') by Robert Louis Stevenson (1850–94);
the line 'And gae his bridle reins a shake' appears in a version of an old
Scottish lyric by Robert Burns (1759–96) published in 1797 as 'It was a'
for our rightfu' king'; 'Love is sweet, love is brief' has not been located,
though may be a misremembering of, for example, 'Love is sweet, and so
are flowers', the first line of 'Love Ephemeral' (from *Verses*, 1847) by
Christina Rossetti (1803–94), or the line 'Life is sweet, love is sweet' from
Rossetti's *The Prince's Progress* (1866); 'Spring, the sweet spring, is the
year's pleasant king,' from a song in *Summers Last Will and Testament*
(1600), a comedy by Thomas Nashe (1567–1601); 'Oh, to be in England |
Now that April's there' are the opening lines of 'Home-Thoughts from
Abroad' (1845) by Robert Browning (1812–89); 'The Three Fishers'
(1851) by Charles Kingsley (1819–75) contains the refrain 'For' or 'But
men must work, and women must weep'; 'The path of duty was the way to

glory' from Tennyson's 'Ode on the Death of the Duke of Wellington' (1852).

'Daughters of England!': from the title of a conduct book for young women by Sarah Ellis, née Stickney (1799–1872): *The Daughters of England: Their Position in Society, Character and Responsibilities* (1842).

Castalia: deriving from the Latin 'chaste' and thus somewhat inappropriate, as Castalia herself will acknowledge, given that she later becomes pregnant.

46 *Dulwich*: a well-to-do area of south-east London, centred around an ancient village long subsumed into the capital, now part of the London Borough of Southwark.

Once . . . the Aloe flowered: the Agave Americana or century plant, also known as the American Aloe though not in fact related to the aloe, was believed to take up to a century to flower. The second book published by Virginia and Leonard Woolf at their Hogarth Press was *Prelude* (1918), a short story by the New Zealand writer Katherine Mansfield (Kathleen Beauchamp Mansfield, 1888–1923); in this story, the young protagonist Kezia asks her mother whether the aloe in their garden flowers, and her mother claims 'Once every hundred years'. Mansfield had entitled a previous version of the story 'The Aloe'. See Katherine Mansfield, *Selected Stories*, ed. Angela Smith, Oxford World's Classics (Oxford: Oxford University Press, 2018), 98, 382.

Sappho: probably born around 620 BCE, Sappho was a Greek poet from the island of Lesbos, whose work was highly revered in classical times. Her lyric poetry survives almost entirely in fragments, notably expressing love and desire between women; the terms 'sapphism' and 'lesbianism' as names for female homosexuality derive from her name and that of her home island.

47 *Cassandra*: according to Greek myth, Cassandra (daughter of King Priam of Troy (see note to p. 45) and his wife Hecuba) was given the gift of true prophecy by the god Apollo in return for her love, but when she refused his advances, he cursed her never to be believed.

48 *'What is chastity then? . . . nothing at all?'*: society's obsession with chastity is a key issue in Woolf's feminist polemic *A Room of One's Own* (1929), in which the narrator suggests 'That profoundly interesting subject, the value that men set upon women's chastity and its effect upon their education, here suggests itself for discussion, and might provide an interesting book if any student at Girton or Newnham cared to go into the matter' (*A Room of One's Own and Three Guineas*, ed. Anna Snaith, Oxford World's Classics (Oxford: Oxford University Press, 2015), 48).

49 *Judith . . . to bear children—*: the biblical Book of Judith (an Apocryphal text in the Protestant and Jewish faiths) recounts how a Jewish widow enabled her city's victory over its attackers by beheading Holofernes, the enemy general, Holofernes having been entranced by her beauty and

invited her into his tent. Judith's sexual allure, plus the ironic quality of the Book of Judith itself, resonate with Woolf's description of potentially liberating advances in reproductive technology, including the provision of free contraception to the public, alongside her satirical allusions to the disquieting eugenicist promotion of selective breeding.

50 *Kensington*: an affluent area of south-west London, adjoining Hyde Park to the north-east. Woolf grew up in Kensington and lived there until early adulthood.

a baronet or only a knight?: in the British system, both a baronet and knight may be called 'Sir', but the former has inherited his title, whereas the latter has had his awarded by the monarch in recognition of merit or service and ranks below a baronet.

Lord Bunkum: another example of Woolf's satirizing of the Establishment: 'bunkum' means nonsense, particularly when spoken by a politician.

51 *Mr Wells . . . Mr Walpole*: all popular writers whose work Woolf herself had reviewed. H. G. Wells (1866–1946) was a prolific and high-profile novelist and polemicist, and an established literary celebrity by the time 'A Society' was published. Woolf had met Wells socially in 1917, and in September 1918 reviewed, somewhat negatively, his novel *Joan and Peter* for the *Times Literary Supplement*; admiring Wells's passionate commitment to ideas, she nevertheless felt that as art, his fiction was lacking, finding his characters formed as 'crude lumps and unmodelled masses' ('The Rights of Youth'; see *The Essays of Virginia Woolf*, ed. Andrew McNeillie (6 vols; London: Hogarth Press, 1986–2011), ii. 293–7, at 296). The work of Arnold Bennett (1867–1931) represented for Woolf what in her view was wrong with contemporary literature; she objected to what she felt was his depthlessly detailed social realism. Woolf wrote 'A Society' as a response to Bennett's *Our Women* (1920), and to Desmond McCarthy's subsequent support in the pages of the *New Statesman* periodical for Bennett's argument that women are intellectually inferior to men. Bennett would be her key target (along with H. G. Wells and a third novelist, John Galsworthy) in her essay 'Character in Fiction' (1924; see *Essays*, iii. 420–38), often now read as a manifesto for Woolf's own early aesthetic principles. Compton Mackenzie (1883–1972) was another highly prolific and popular novelist, now best remembered for *Whiskey Galore* (1947). By the time Woolf wrote 'A Society' he had already made his literary reputation with *Sinister Street* (1913–14); she had also reviewed, somewhat satirically, his *Sylvia Scarlett* (1918) and *Sylvia and Michael* (1919) (see *Essays*, ii. 288–91 and 20–1 respectively). Woolf reviewed *Sonia Married* (1919), by Stephen McKenna (1888–1967) (see *Essays*, iii. 95–6); the novel was a sequel to his most famous work *Sonia: Between Two Worlds* (1917). The popular novelist Hugh Walpole (1884–1941) became a great friend of Woolf's in the 1930s; although she did not always admire his work, she warmly reviewed his novel *The Green Mirror* in 1918 (see *Essays*, ii. 214–17).

'War! War! War! Declaration of War!': Britain declared war on Germany on 4 August 1914.

52 *In 1760 . . . In 1900 on the other hand—*: 1760 was the midpoint of the Seven Years War (1756–63) between Britain and Prussia (now part of Germany) on one side and France, Austria, Russia, Sweden, and Saxony (the last also now part of Germany) on the other. After centuries of decline, the Venetian Republic fell on 12 May 1797, under threat of attack from French forces as part of the Revolutionary Wars. Napoleon Bonaparte declared himself 'Emperor of the French' on 2 December 1804. None of these dates mark the most significant military events in either period. The 'Seven Week' or Austro-Prussian War took place in the summer of 1866; the Franco-Prussian War lasted from 1870 to 1871; both wars were part of the campaign for German unification, declared on 18 January 1871. The Boxer Rebellion, a Chinese government-sanctioned peasant uprising against foreigners and Chinese converts to Christianity, was effectively brought to an end when international forces captured the capital Beijing on 14 August 1900.

Mr Lloyd George: David Lloyd George (1863–1945), Liberal prime minister of the United Kingdom between 1916 and 1922. Although celebrated in his lifetime as 'the man who won the war', by 1920 he was already widely reviled, under attack from his own party as well as political opponents on left and right.

53 *'How could they help it? . . . It's all our doing!'*: a further prefiguring of Woolf's ironic commentary on patriarchy in *A Room of One's Own* (see note to p. 48), in which she says 'Women have served all these centuries as looking-glasses possessing the magic and delicious power of reflecting the figure of man at twice its natural size' (*A Room of One's Own*, ed. Snaith, 28).

the Treaty of Peace had just been signed: the Treaty of Versailles; see note to p. 16.

54 *Evening News*: the first popular evening newspaper in London, aimed at a wide reading public and by this time one of the most successful newspapers in the country.

IN THE ORCHARD

55 *'Ce pays . . . le mieux . . .'*: (French) 'This country is truly one of the corners of the world where the laughter of girls breaks out most easily . . .'. From *Ramuntcho* (1897), a love and adventure story set in the Basque region of France by the French novelist and naval officer Pierre Loti (pseudonym for Julien Viaud, 1850–1923).

Hymns Ancient and Modern: the standard hymn-book adopted by the Church of England since its publication in 1861.

churched: attending a religious ceremony of purification and thanksgiving after giving birth.

golden feather of the church tower: the weathervane.

A WOMAN'S COLLEGE FROM OUTSIDE

58 *The feathery-white moon . . . in the meadows*: a first draft of what was to become 'A Woman's College from Outside' appears in the manuscript of Woolf's 1922 novel *Jacob's Room*; this phrase is all that remains of that draft in the published version of *Jacob's Room* (see Introduction, pp. xviii, xix–xx).

Tartary: once used by Europeans as a blanket term for the area of central Asia stretching east from the Caspian Sea to the Pacific Ocean; already an archaism by the early twentieth century.

Newnham: along with Girton, one of the two first women-only colleges of the University of Cambridge, after lectures for women began in 1870. Founded in 1871 as a residence for female students, it was established on its present site in 1875.

60 *Bamborough Castle*: now usually spelt 'Bamburgh', a castle on the northeast English coast, close to the border with Scotland.

THE NEW DRESS

61 *Borrow or Scott*: George Borrow (1803–81), English novelist and travel writer; Sir Walter Scott (1771–1832), Edinburgh-born poet and novelist; both favourites of Woolf's.

a Paris fashion book of the time of the Empire: given Mabel's apparent age (around 40, see p. 67), this must be the Second Empire (1852–70). Woolf was photographed for *Vogue* in May 1924 (aged 42) wearing a dress of her mother's; the photograph was reproduced at the end of 'A Woman's College from Outside' in its first publication in *Atalanta's Garland* (see Introduction, p. xviii).

62 *We are all like flies . . . 'Flies trying to crawl,' she repeated*: one of a number of allusions in this story to *The Duel* (1891), a novella by the Russian writer Anton Chekhov (1860–1904), in which a character describes herself as 'like a fly that has fallen into the inkpot [. . .] she kept falling into the ink and crawling out into the light again' (Anton Tchehov, *The Tales of Tchehov*, ii. *The Duel and Other Stories*, trans. Constance Garnett (London: Chatto and Windus, 1916), 105, 108); see also note to p. 63. Woolf may also have had in mind the 1922 short story 'The Fly' by Katherine Mansfield (see note to p. 46), in which a man drowns a fly in ink (Mansfield, *Selected Stories*, ed. Smith, 357–61). In neither story, however, does the fly try to escape from a saucer.

63 *'Lies, lies, lies!'*: *The Duel* (see note to p. 62) contains the line 'Lies, lies, lies. . . .' (*The Tales of Tchehov*, trans. Garnett, ii. 133).

scrolloping: an invention of Woolf's; all six examples of this word in the *Oxford English Dictionary* are from her works.

64 *Boadicea*: now more usually known as Boudicca, queen of a British Celtic tribe who led a rebellion against the occupying Roman forces in 60 CE.

65 *three penny bit*: a very small silver coin, having a diameter of 16 millimetres (5/8 inch).

66 *some hero like Sir Henry Lawrence*: Sir Henry Montgomery Lawrence (1806–57) was an army officer in the British East India Company who died defending the city of Lucknow during the Indian Rebellion, an uprising against the company which at that time governed much of India on behalf of the British Crown.

67 *the Strand*: one of central London's main thoroughfares, so named because it originally skirted the river Thames.

'SLATER'S PINS HAVE NO POINTS'

69 *'SLATER'S PINS HAVE NO POINTS'*: when republished in the collection *A Haunted House* (1944) edited by Leonard Woolf after Virginia's death, this story was entitled 'Moments of Being: "Slater's Pins Have No Points"', restoring the first half of the title as it appeared in the typescript of this story.

Bach fugue: the German composer Johann Sebastian Bach (1685–1750) was well known for his fugues, polyphonic compositions built around one or more subjects or themes, and characterized by the use of imitative counterpoint.

the Archer Street College of Music: there is an Archer Street in Soho, central London, but no record of a college of music there. Archer Street was, however, an important meeting point for musicians from the 1920s onwards because of its proximity to theatres and clubs (both the Apollo and the Lyric theatres had doors opening onto it) and places to drink. The London Orchestral Association had its headquarters in Archer Street; known as the Club it had a licensed bar and downstairs changing facilities where requests for musicians for particular performances might be left. With many thanks to Rowena Anketell for this information.

Salisbury: a cathedral city in Wiltshire, south-west England.

72 *Browning*: Robert Browning (1812–89), celebrated English poet and playwright.

Serpentine: a recreational lake in London's Hyde Park.

Avon: there are three rivers named the Avon in England: the Bristol Avon, the Warwickshire Avon (also known as Shakespeare's Avon since it passes through his birthplace), and the Salisbury or Hampshire Avon.

the Bridge: the Serpentine Bridge, which marks the boundary between Hyde Park and Kensington Gardens.

Ravenna: a city in north-east Italy.

73 *Hampton Court*: begun in 1514 by Cardinal Wolsey, on the banks of the Thames south-west of London, and confiscated by Henry VIII in the late 1520s, Hampton Court Palace was opened to the public in 1838 and by the

early twentieth century was one of England's most popular tourist attractions; Woolf herself visited frequently.

73 *Waterloo*: London railway terminus for trains to the south and south-west.

Brompton Road: a central London thoroughfare in the Royal Borough of Kensington and Chelsea, famous as the location for the luxury department store Harrods.

The Oxford World's Classics Website

www.worldsclassics.co.uk

- Browse the full range of Oxford World's Classics online

- Sign up for our monthly e-alert to receive information on new titles

- Read extracts from the Introductions

- Listen to our editors and translators talk about the world's greatest literature with our Oxford World's Classics audio guides

- Join the conversation, follow us on Twitter at OWC_Oxford

- Teachers and lecturers can order inspection copies quickly and simply via our website

www.worldsclassics.co.uk

American Literature

British and Irish Literature

Children's Literature

Classics and Ancient Literature

Colonial Literature

Eastern Literature

European Literature

Gothic Literature

History

Medieval Literature

Oxford English Drama

Philosophy

Poetry

Politics

Religion

The Oxford Shakespeare

A complete list of Oxford World's Classics, including Authors in Context, Oxford English Drama, and the Oxford Shakespeare, is available in the UK from the Marketing Services Department, Oxford University Press, Great Clarendon Street, Oxford OX2 6DP, or visit the website at www.oup.com/uk/worldsclassics.

In the USA, visit www.oup.com/us/owc for a complete title list.

Oxford World's Classics are available from all good bookshops. In case of difficulty, customers in the UK should contact Oxford University Press Bookshop, 116 High Street, Oxford OX1 4BR.

HENRY ADAMS	**The Education of Henry Adams**
LOUISA MAY ALCOTT	**Little Women**
SHERWOOD ANDERSON	**Winesburg, Ohio**
EDWARD BELLAMY	**Looking Backward 2000–1887**
CHARLES BROCKDEN BROWN	**Wieland; or The Transformation and Memoirs of Carwin, The Biloquist**
WILLA CATHER	**My Ántonia** **O Pioneers!**
KATE CHOPIN	**The Awakening and Other Stories**
JAMES FENIMORE COOPER	**The Last of the Mohicans**
STEPHEN CRANE	**The Red Badge of Courage**
J. HECTOR ST. JEAN DE CRÈVECŒUR	**Letters from an American Farmer**
FREDERICK DOUGLASS	**Narrative of the Life of Frederick Douglass, an American Slave**
THEODORE DREISER	**Sister Carrie**
F. SCOTT FITZGERALD	**The Great Gatsby** **The Beautiful and Damned** **Tales of the Jazz Age** **This Side of Paradise**
BENJAMIN FRANKLIN	**Autobiography and Other Writings**
CHARLOTTE PERKINS GILMAN	**The Yellow Wall-Paper and Other Stories**
ZANE GREY	**Riders of the Purple Sage**
NATHANIEL HAWTHORNE	**The Blithedale Romance** **The House of the Seven Gables** **The Marble Faun** **The Scarlet Letter** **Young Goodman Brown and Other Tales**